The Hunt

The Hunt

Dr. H

ISBN: 9798985718317

Acknowledgements:

This book is a work of fiction. The characters and events are a creation of the author. Certain locations mentioned in this book exist. Their names and locations are the results of several discussions with the author's in-laws who have resided in Key Marathon for the past fifty years.

The author would like to thank the Good Lord for assisting me in the creation of this novel. He also would like to thank his wife of fifty years who assisted in the writing and editing of this novel. In addition, he would like to thank the Hill families, who contributed to identifying various locations in Marathon, the Shuman and Laszakovits families who assisted in the editing of this book, the Malone family whose son created the hydrodynamics theory on the impacts of hurricanes in the Florida Keys, the Pelican family, specifically my daughter who assisted in the various Spanish translations. The author would like to thank the homicide squads in the Amarillo Police Department and Sergeant Colby Doaks, Criminal Investigations Division, Randall County Sheriff's

Department who have guided me through the intricacies of evolving forensics applied in homicide scene investigations, and Eric Jones for information on a Fusion Center operations. Finally, the author would like to thank Steven Bigham who greatly contributed to pointing the author into the world of drones and weapons used now in modern warfare.

May God Bless all the readers of this book. Thanks Harry

Chapter One:

The Unknown Identical Twin

September 13, 2021

We were waiting for a conference call from our medical examiner, Dr. Spock. Over the past two weeks, we had heard rumors of the possibility that our murder suspect, Maria Hernandez, was not killed during a raid on her residences. Originally Dr. Spock had confirmed that the body found at the raid scene was that of Maria Hernandez. However, Spock found that the fingerprints on this body were not those of Maria Hernandez but her identical twin sister. Now Spock would tell our homicide squad why he had to *change* his autopsy report. One of the reasons for this change was because he had *no hits* on the fingerprints of the dead woman he autopsied from any local, state, or national fingerprint data systems. Maria had her fingerprints on file with the Department of Public Safety for prior arrests. When these prints from Maria came back without a hit, he sent the fingerprints to Interpol. There the prints were identified by Interpol and another country's police department as those of Selena Rodriguez

Today Spock would tell us that he now knows that the dead body at the crime scene was Maria's identical twin sister, a person no one had known about until today. Consequently, we learned that Maria is probably alive and living somewhere in the world. I respected Dr. Spock, but I wondered, *How could Dr. Spock miss identifying the body as Maria Hernandez, then two weeks later change his findings?* Just hearing about this rumor was most frustrating to all our homicide squad members, but especially for Sgt. Doaks—my supervisor—and me. For the past three weeks, we had developed numerous leads pointing to Maria Hernandez as a key suspect in seven homicides over the past twenty years. We had been going to arrest her two weeks ago, but the IRS and other federal and state agencies delayed our actions. Why? They had developed enough probable cause to execute several search warrants on her residences in Key Marathon. When this raid on Maria's residences occurred, Doaks and I were on a Coast Guard Cutter. We had thought that Maria was killed at this crime scene. Now we would learn from Spock how the dead woman's body at this crime scene was not Maria Hernandez, but her twin sister Selena. *Maria had escaped!*

My name is Katie Hood. I am a thirty-five-year-old, single female detective working for the Homicide Unit in the Mangrove County Sheriff's Department in Key Marathon. I started my career in law enforcement in 2007 as a patrol officer in Key West. There I saw what people can do to one another in committing various personal and property crimes. I left the Key West Police Department in 2014 and became a deputy in the Mangrove County Sheriff's Department. At first I was assigned to the jail; then I was reassigned to patrol duty for about four years. After that I tested and was promoted to detective in property crimes. Eighteen months later I was assigned to homicide. My current assignment has provided me with great opportunities to use new forensic tools and techniques. I work with my partner and supervisor, Sgt. Doaks. Doaks is old school—a piece of work as a detective. He hates using any forensic tools and computers. He has been a cop for over thirty years and solves homicides the old-fashioned way: with lots of investigative work. He is my supervisor and is a royal pain in my hind parts. He knows a lot about the people and the culture of the Keys and has helped me solve a number of homicides in the past several years. He always reminds me of his experiences working the street, telling me, "You develop a gut instinct for crimes, suspects, and crime scenes."

While waiting for Spock's phone call, my eyes looked over at my partner. His physical characteristics are those of an older man—in his fifties, overweight, does not work out. He eats whatever food he wants, has been divorced twice, and is a borderline alcoholic. He has been with the sheriff's department for a long time—over thirty years. But I must admit, he has helped me solve a number of homicides in my career, so I do respect him. While waiting for this phone call today, my mind replayed the results of the state police investigation into the battle occurring at the Hut on August 25. The morning of the raid had turned deadly. Ten police officers were killed, twenty more were wounded, and six civilians were killed. Our key suspect, Maria Hernandez, was supposedly killed at the scene, but today our medical examiner was going to confirm that Maria was *not* one of the deceased.

At 2:00 p.m. Dr. Spock began his conference call by stating that the body he had originally identified as Maria Hernandez killed at the raid two weeks ago was *not* in fact Maria Hernandez. He explained how he pulled up Maria's driver's license picture to verify it was her. He compared the woman's face to Maria's driver's license. They looked identical.

His first thought was that Maria was killed. However, he said, "On August 29, 2021, when I ran the fingerprints through AFIS (automatic fingerprint identification system), there was no match. I knew Maria had been arrested in the past and her prints should have been on file. But when nothing came back from AFIS, I expanded my search through Interpol. Interpol identified these fingerprints as belonging to Selena Rodriquez living in Seville, Spain." He continued, "In addition, I noted that the body had a number of scars and tattoos, which Interpol confirmed was Selena Rodriquez. Now I believe Selena was a person *none* of the law enforcement community knew about until now. I will be amending my autopsy report to reflect the correct identification as Selena Rodriquez. One other thing: Selena was pregnant at the time of her death, and she had ingested some drug. I am waiting on our final lab report to confirm what type of drug." Dr. Spock then asked if anyone had any questions. For the next several seconds, no one talked. Everyone was looking at each other, and all had one question no one was willing to ask: Who the h- -l is Selena Rodriquez from Seville, Spain?

Doaks finally spoke up and asked Dr. Spock, "Are you sure about your findings now?"

Spock responded, "Yes, given the information from Interpol and then from the National Police of Spain—plus the body scars and tattoos—I am now convinced that Selena Rodriguez was killed in our raid. In addition, I learned she was under investigation as a prime suspect in the homicides of several wealthy men in Europe. Currently, she is under investigation for selling classified information on the locations of sunken Spanish treasure ships around the Florida Keys. Both Interpol and the National Police of Spain want to speak to any U.S. police agency involved in her death. Any other questions?" Dr. Spock asked. No one responded, and Dr. Spock hung up. *Crud, crud, crud*, I told myself. My mind was racing—who in the world was this Selena? Why didn't we know about her? When Dr. Spock notified our unit about all the people killed at the raid on the property of Maria Hernandez, I had assumed that the body was Maria Hernandez. If Selena was anything like her sister, Maria, I was glad she was dead. Maria was a ruthless crime lord managing all types of crimes in the Florida Keys. I vividly remember how Sgt. Doaks and I originally got a lead on our murder suspect: Maria Hernandez. On August 18, working with my uncle, we dug up a body on the beach near a restaurant called *the Hut*. While we were digging up one body, I called in a cadaver dog. The dog arrived and alerted on additional possible bodies under the grave of our first victim. We later found two babies' bodies buried there.

I began daydreaming about that day. It was a great sunny day in Key Marathon. I was lobster diving with my family when my Uncle Harry called me to come to the Hut shoreline due to the odor of a possible dead human body. Later that day we found our first victim. We identified the first body as Jack Kennedy. Unfortunately, we also found two more bodies under the grave of our first victim. These bodies were wrapped in two Styrofoam boxes, and we identified them as two infants. Unfortunately, we are still awaiting the DNA results on these two babies. Our victim, Jack Kennedy, was identified by his fingerprints through a search of the crime records of DPS (Department of Public Safety) and NCIC (National Crime Information Center). After identifying the victim as Jack Kennedy, five other Florida police departments using these databases had alerted us that Kennedy was a suspect in several murders, embezzlements, and drug cases in Florida.

My mind was still daydreaming about that day when Doaks yelled at me. "Rookie! Let's get to work on the updated information Dr. Spock just gave our squad."

Doaks stood up after Spock hung up and addressed our homicide squad. "Well, s- - t, now we need to reopen our investigation. First, I think we need to do a background investigation on Selena Rodriquez. Next, we need to find out where in the world is Maria Hernandez?" He was about to continue when the sheriff entered the room.

Doaks sat down and the sheriff spoke: "I just found out about this Selena Rodriquez person. I am shocked about this finding. As a result, I will be needing your assistance in the next few days as I am planning to put together a multi-level task force whose sole purpose is to find Maria Hernandez. Currently I am working with our DPS, the IRS, the FBI, and the Office of Homeland Security in organizing this joint task force. I will get back to you in the next few days once these agencies agree on everyone's roles in this new work party. Thank you." Then the sheriff left the squad room.

At 3:30 p.m. the sheriff called Sgt. Doaks and me into his office for a meeting. We entered and were introduced to FBI Special Agent Stone O'Neill. We all shook hands and sat down. The sheriff told us that Agent O'Neill would be working with our department. He wanted to give us some additional information on Maria Hernandez. O'Neill began telling us about another raid that occurred on the same date and time on another associate of Maria Hernandez.

"On August 25 around 6:00 a.m., another raid was executed on the office and residence of Juan Perez living in Key West. Juan, a certified public accountant (CPA), had been filing Maria's income tax returns in Florida and her federal income tax returns over the past decade. Once the police began to serve the search warrants on Maria's residences in Marathon Key, two special squads from the FBI and DPS insertion teams served search warrants on Mr. Perez's business and his home in Key West."

O'Neill continued, "The search of his business provided detailed documents showing how Maria had sequestered millions of dollars into numerous offshore accounts in the Cayman and the British Virgin Islands. These accounts were created in January 1999 and had considerable capital gains over the past twenty-two years. The insertion team serving the warrants at Juan Perez's home got into a major gun battle. As this unit was about to knock on the door of Juan Perez, they were fired upon from three different locations. One person was inside the front door entrance. A second person was hidden in the attic of the suspect's house, and the third person firing was exiting the area in a speed boat. A gun battle began and lasted about fifteen minutes. The two people inside the house were killed when the insertion team returned fire. The third individual was escaping the house on a boat when a Coast Guard helicopter opened fire. The boat exploded, and the individual in it was obliterated in the explosion. The house was subsequently searched. The search revealed a wall safe. The safe was opened, and in it were a number of receipts from Maria Hernandez that were paid to a Selena Rodriquez for services rendered over the past eighteen months. These receipts amounted to 15 million dollars. These items were seized and given to the IRS and DPS Commanders following both searches. As of this date, the dead people have not been identified."

Agent O'Neill stopped and asked us if we had any questions. Doaks said no, but I wanted to know who was doing the follow-up investigations on Perez and whether we could continue our murder investigation on Maria Hernandez. The sheriff spoke up: "Hood, your questions are good, but we cannot answer them yet. I am still in the process of putting together this multi-level task force. Once that is formed, you will be able to ask the commander of this task force any questions you have. Do you understand?" the sheriff asked.

"Yes, sir!" I exclaimed, then shut up.

Both men stood up. Doaks and I stood up as well, thanking Agent O'Neill before leaving the sheriff's office.

"Well, crap," I told Doaks. "Why were we the only two detectives called into that meeting?" Doaks looked at me, then at the ceiling, and stated, "I think the sheriff wanted to make us feel special after all the work and violence we have gone through over the past weeks." He continued, "I don't like working with the feds; they control everything and are the ones—and I mean the only ones—who get all the credit in solving their cases. I am very worried how much real police work you and I will be able to do if we are assigned to this task force."

"Time to go off duty," I yelled at Doaks. "Tomorrow is another day."

As I was about to leave my office, Agent O'Neill appeared

at my door. "Can I buy you and Doaks dinner tonight?" That's a first, I thought. An FBI agent, not too bad looking, asking me and Doaks if he can buy dinner!

"Sure, let me check with Doaks first. Can you stay here for one minute?" I asked.

"Yes," O'Neill said.

I took off trying to find Doaks. First stop was his office—not there—then the men's room. "Doaks, Doaks, are you in there?" I yelled.

"Hood, what the h - -l! Can I just get some peace and quiet without you disturbing me?" he blabbered.

"Listen," I told him. "That FBI agent O'Neill wants to buy us dinner and probably pick our brains on what we found after the shootout on Maria's properties, so are you interested?" I asked.

"Sure," he yelled, "H - -l yeah, let's spend the fed's money! Does the Island Fish Company sound OK with you?"

"Absolutely," I chuckled. "I hear they have excellent lobster."

"Great," Doaks said. "Let's go and you can tell Agent O'Neill where he can meet us." O'Neill was ready to go, so we all left for the Island Fish Company.

The evening at this restaurant was perfect. A soft breeze was coming off the Gulf, boats were tied to the docks adjacent to the restaurant, the temperature was warm, and the restaurant was not busy. O'Neill asked the hostess to put us in a secluded room if possible. He slipped her a twenty-dollar bill to make sure it was a secluded location. Doaks winked at me and shook his head. "Big spender," he whispered in my ear. *Good*, I thought, *I'm starving. I am going to have a big meal tonight on Uncle Sam.*

After we sat down, O'Neill stated, "We can order drinks if we want, but it would have to be on a separate tab." I promptly ordered a glass of Moscato, Doaks ordered a Crown and Coke, and O'Neill ordered a Maker's Mark on the rocks. After drinks were served and dinner was ordered, O'Neill motioned for both of us to lean onto the table. We did; then he stated, "If possible, I want to hear from both of you in detail on what you found at the crime scenes on Maria's properties. Then I want to pick your brains about some possible locations where Maria might have gone." For a moment there was a long silence. Then Doaks looked at me and back at O'Neill, took a long swig, and said to O'Neill, "Let me start by telling you what we found."

For the next two hours, we unloaded on him.

Chapter Two:

Recalling the War Zone

Doaks started his recollection of the events which occurred on August 25th and 26. He told O'Neill that he had read the final after-action report on this raid. Then he went into some very specific details. "On Wednesday morning at 6:00 a.m., three tactical squads made up of twenty SWAT officers per squad began their approach toward the doors at three residences owned by Maria Hernandez. At 6:01 a.m. Alpha Team approached the front door of the Hut restaurant, while Bravo Team and Charlie Team approached the east and west doors on the two high-rise apartment buildings. As all three teams silently approached each of these three breaching locations, a hailstorm of automatic weapons fire erupted from the basement of the two high-rise apartment buildings and from the second-floor landing above the entrance to the Hut. Within seconds all the tactical squads were under attack. As the teams moved into covered positions and began to return fire, three officers from each of the squads made their approach to breaching the three door locations. Once they got inside a ten-foot radius of the doors, claymore mines exploded—killing all of these officers. The firefight continued for the next ten minutes. Then more cops attempted to breach these doors, but again they were met with a firestorm from a number of automatic weapons. As the gun battles continued, the pilots controlling the two-armed Coast Guard helicopters hovering above this location lowered their flying altitudes to engage the suspects firing from the underground garage in both high-rise apartments. Once both helicopters opened fire, they were immediately attacked from other positions located in both penthouses on the top floor of each high-rise apartment. Miraculously, although both were hit, they were able to return fire and rise to a higher altitude. This firefight continued for another five minutes. None of the tactical teams were able to breach their door locations in all three buildings. More claymore mines exploded, and the firefight continued. Once the helicopter reached a higher altitude, its machine guns opened fire again, killing the penthouse gunmen. Then the tactical squads began clearing all the areas and finally made entry into all of Maria's properties."

Doaks continued his story. "After the raid was over, we believed Maria was killed at the Hut. The next day, August 26, Hood and I walked the grid on this horrible crime scene. We knew that ten SWAT officers and a number of civilian personnel were killed. Twenty other officers were wounded, several still fighting for their lives. Later we were told this was one of the deadliest days for Florida police officers in the history of the state. As we were walking the grid, both of us had an extremely tough time holding ourselves together. We could see evidence of dried blood and claymore mine shrapnel along the Atlantic Ocean side of the high-rise apartments. Looking at this crime scene, Hood and I got a true sense of a war zone. The blast patterns from the claymores, the bullet patterns in the trees and on the buildings, and the shrapnel evidence left me speechless. Hood and I had tears streaming down our faces. Death is the ultimate sacrifice facing every police officer every day in America. The crime scene was huge—about four hundred yards along the beach—then the high-rise apartment complex was five stories tall with forty separate rooms. Then in the basement garage, there was another crime scene. There some more evidence was found where several improvised explosive devices (IEDs) were placed by someone escaping the area. More evidence was found where several burn bags were ignited in the north side of the underground garage."

Doaks paused, then continued, "Hood and I looked at this garage scene and immediately had one question: who did this?" (That question would come back and haunt us for the next months.) Doaks resumed his story about the evidence we found in the garbage disposal in Maria's kitchen later the same day. Then he told O'Neill about the secret passageway he found in the hallway. He left out the parts where I grabbed him and ordered him not to go into the passageway—let the bomb squad check for IEDs.

Once Doaks was finished, O'Neill thanked him for his detailed report. I had nothing to add. Then the FBI agent told us, "Maria sounds like a drug lord or some type of organized crime leader. The amount of firepower, the use of IEDs, and claymores tells me she has access to firepower even law enforcement would struggle to own."

"You hit the nail on the head," Doaks stated. "I have talked to all of the squad sergeants running these operations. They all stated that they had never encountered the onslaught of automatic weapons fire like they encountered on this raid."

O'Neill then asked, "How does Commander Juan Lopez fit into the escape of Maria?" Doaks just about spit out his drink, trying to answer that question.

I jumped in. "That is a huge sore spot and embarrassment to our department. The sheriff has an ongoing internal affairs investigation into two moles we discovered during our homicide investigation. Both were possibly related to Maria. Somehow, both were undetected until we identified a key eyewitness in the Kennedy homicide case, then the extent of Maria's intelligence was discovered," I continued.

But O'Neill interrupted, "How did Maria's intelligence know all of this?"

Doaks had now recovered and jumped in himself. "The b - -h tried to kill us three times. She knew we had a key eyewitness in our protective custody. Her attacks were aimed to kill him!" Doaks stated.

"Three times?" O'Neill questioned.

"Yes, three times," Doaks croaked. He then proceeded to tell O'Neill all the details about the attacks on our safe houses, then on the Coast Guard Cutter.

"Damn," O'Neill whispered. "What the h - -l! How did she know all of these locations and your plans?"

"We figured Commander Lopez and a dispatch supervisor had helped her identify all of these locations. The sheriff just validated this information last week. Now we have an APB (all-points bulletin) out on Lopez. The dispatch supervisor committed suicide last week. With your help, we want to create a red notice—a global arrest warrant for suspects committing serious crimes—through Interpol. We also think both Lopez and Hernandez may have hooked up outside the country and may be starting a new criminal organization somewhere in the world," Doaks concluded.

O'Neill just sat there staring out into the Gulf. I could see he had a lot of things he was sorting out, but he didn't say anything at first. Then he turned to both of us and said, "Thank you both for sharing. I appreciate your work, and I am sorry for your heavy losses. I would like to continue our conversation later this week. I have some background infor-mation I need to complete in getting the red notices created on Juan Lopez and Maria Hernandez. I will get the dinner tab so we can all leave now." He got up and took the bill to the cashier.

Doaks and I looked at each other. Then Doaks stated,

"Do you think we can work with him?"

I did not answer him right away. I then said, "I am willing to work with him because he seems genuine and concerned about getting Maria and her sidekick, Lopez."

Doaks' answer was noncommittal. "I am not going to trust him yet. He has to prove to me that he is willing to work with you and me and our sheriff." On that note, Doaks and I left the restaurant. As I was leaving, I began to wonder—there was something different about O'Neill, but I couldn't put my finger on it just yet.

Chapter Three:

The National Police Corps and Selena Rodriquez

September 14, 2021

Doaks and I met in his office to discuss any updated information following the Selena Rodriquez death investigation. Doaks handed me an updated police report on the raid from the Department of Public Safety, Special Investigations Unit. I read over the report and took a deep breath. My prayers went out to the families of all of these officers. Line-of-duty deaths are one of the hardest parts of a cop's job. I had been through several deaths in my career as a police officer, here and in Key West. Police funerals are the worst. Seeing the families, the kids, and all of the sadness brought back a lot of memories. I said a quick prayer to the Good Lord asking Him to heal those officers fighting for their lives now and to continue to bless those officers' families killed in this incident. I closed my eyes and thought, *Where is Maria Hernandez?* I vowed that my next year would be dedicated to finding this woman and making her pay for all of the lives of our cops and citizens she had killed in the past three decades.

I gave the report back to Doaks and asked, "What's next for us?"

He stated, "Let's review our interview with Sam Decree. I think we have covered all the bases, but let's call D.A. Moceri to see if there may be something we are missing to complete our investigation on Hernandez to date."

I thought back to when all three of us were on the Coast Guard Cutter trying not to get killed by Maria Hernandez. While there, Doaks and I spent ten hours interviewing Sam Decree. He was in protective custody under our control during those days (which seemed like years). Decree's statements had been read and approved by our district attorney, Don Moceri. He was ready to go to the Grand Jury to indict Maria Hernandez on several counts of murder. But since Maria had escaped our country, these indictments had to wait until our department—or a federal agency—located and returned Maria Hernandez to the Keys. Maria's location in the world was unknown while Sam Decree had a new life in a federal witness protection program.

Doaks reminded me to contact the Cocoa Beach Police Chief to see if we could reschedule the use of his ground penetrating radar in a few weeks. I had arranged with Clutch, the assistant director of DPS in Florida, to have this tool delivered on the same day the warrants were executed at Maria Hernandez's residences. But these plans were canceled because of the extensive crime scenes resulting from the gun battles with Selena Rodriquez. I thought that now was the time to conclude our homicide investigation at the Hut. Doaks agreed. He too wanted to find out how many more bodies may be buried in the sand by the seawall at the Hut. I told Doaks I would get on it this afternoon, but first I was going to get some coffee.

The call from the National Police Corps Headquarters in Spain came on Sgt. Doaks' phone at about 10:30 a.m. Doaks took the call. On the phone, a man identified as Colonel Ortez wanted to speak to the homicide supervisor. Doaks put the call on speaker.

"Hello, this is Colonel Ortez from the National Police Headquarters in Seville, Spain. Who am I speaking to now?" he asked.

"This is Sgt. Doaks, supervisor of the homicide unit in the Mangrove County Sheriff's Office," Doaks explained. For the next five minutes, Colonel Ortez spoke nonstop to Doaks. The Colonel wanted to know everything we had done on the investigation of Selena Rodriquez. Doaks then explained that we had just learned the results of the autopsy on a body the coroner originally thought was Maria Hernandez. At this time, our department had just started a new investigation involving Selena Rodriquez.

The Colonel was silent for a moment. Then he asked Doaks, "So, for the past two weeks, you did not know the body in the morgue was Selena Rodriquez?"

"No," Doaks replied, "we just received notification on

whose body was in the morgue yesterday."

The Colonel sighed. Then he stated, "I need to clarify one thing. Are you going to be the primary detective working the criminal investigation on Selena Rodriquez?"

"Yes," Doaks replied. The Colonel then asked if he could email Sgt. Doaks several attachments regarding his department's investigations on Selena to date. Doaks responded yes, then gave him his cellphone and email address. He also gave him my name, office number, and email address. The Colonel wrote down all of the email addresses and phone numbers, then asked Doaks what time it was in the Keys. Doaks told him it was currently 11:00 a.m. The Colonel said that in Spain it was 6:00 p.m., so there was a seven-hour difference. The Colonel then asked, "Can you and your homicide squad review the background materials I'm sending?"

Doaks replied, "We could have these all read and have another conference call tomorrow morning."

Ortez agreed and arranged to have a conference call the next morning at around 8:00 a.m. Key West time.

Doaks then asked the colonel, "How many pages are there in your background investigation reports, and are they written in Spanish or English?"

The colonel stated something in Spanish, then apologized to Doaks. "Sgt. Doaks, my apologies," he said. "There are about ten pages in each report, and all are written in Spanish. Do you have someone at your sheriff's office who could translate these reports, or would you prefer that we have our reports translated into English?"

Doaks then asked the colonel an unusual question. "Colonel, are the reports written in Castilian or in Andalusian?"

The colonel responded, "Excellent question, my friend. They are written in the Castilian dialect."

Doaks stated, "Then, Colonel, could your department please translate them since our Spanish dialect here is substantially different?"

"Absolutely! We will get them translated today, and I will email these reports to you later this evening."

"Thank you, Colonel. Is there anything I can provide to you and your agency as we begin this investigation in the United States?" asked Doaks.

"No, my friend. I like the way you think, and I appreciate your cooperation. I will have these reports translated and sent to you within the next three hours. Thank you again, and goodbye." said the colonel.

Doaks hung up the phone. I looked at him and asked, "How did you know about the different dialects of Spanish in Spain?"

"Another secret of mine you just learned—and there is a lot more to Doaks than his thirty-plus years in police work and his love for food." With that, Doaks left the area and went to the restroom. I mumbled to myself, "What else is Doaks keeping from me?" Then I left the area and went to my office. I was just about to call the Police Chief in Cocoa Beach when Doaks rushed into my office. "Rookie, I just got the first report from the cops in Spain. You will not believe what this Selena has done!" Doaks exclaimed.

"Is she as bad as her twin sister?" I asked.

"Worse—I think they both could have set up a global crime network if they hadn't known about each other until three years ago," Doaks explained. For the next hour, Doaks and I read over the investigative reports on Selena Rodriquez.

"Wow! She and Maria were cut out of the same cloth," I stated. Both were extremely cunning and dangerous at an early age. Maria liked her money, but Selena liked her men, and it appeared she liked to kill them and take their money.

"Interesting!" Doaks exclaimed. "Maria was into embezzling her money, but we just couldn't prove anything involving her when we arrested her husband. According to the cops in Spain, Selena liked her men and their money. The cops in Spain have her listed as a prime suspect in five homicides but could not find enough conclusive evidence to tie her to any one of these homicides."

"Reminds me of our case with Maria and her handgun," I stated. "We have seven homicides directly related to her weapon but no luck in finding where that weapon is located yet," I sighed. I looked away for a second, then asked Doaks, "Where do you think Maria is right now?"

"I have been asking myself that same question since we learned about Selena," he said. "Somehow I think Maria and Juan Lopez are connected, but I just can't prove it yet."

I looked at Doaks, then asked him another question. "Has

anyone done any investigations into the connection between Lopez and Hernandez?"

Doaks looked at me and said, "No one has done that investigation yet. Is that something you want to do?"

I thought about my answer for a few moments. Considering that our homicide department was going to be involved in a newly formed task force, I thought about the loose ends in our Kennedy investigation. "I need your advice on this question before I answer it, ok?" I asked.

Doaks looked at me, then frowned. "Let me get this straight. You are asking for my advice on something?"

"Yes. Go ahead and mark this day on your calendar because there won't be many," I laughed.

"OK, Rookie, what do you need?" he stated.

"In your opinion, what are your predictions on our roles in this evolving task force investigating this case?" I asked.

"Well, I am not sure. I know we have a lot of loose ends on the Kennedy homicide, and we need to finish our search at the Hut for more buried bodies. And frankly, I don't know what kind of investigations we may coordinate with the National Police Corps in Spain on Selena," he said. I nodded my head and agreed with him.

I said, "I guess I was a little worried about trying to do another investigation involving Lopez and Hernandez while continuing our Kennedy investigation." Doaks nodded his head, agreeing, and we continued reading the reports from the cops in Spain. Little did I know that within the next day, all of my questions would be answered—and many other areas of this investigation would explode.

Chapter Four:

Selena Rodriquez and the National Police Corps

September 15, 2021

The call from Colonel Ortez came in at 8:00 a.m. Doaks pushed the phone button to speaker mode so that he, the sheriff, the chief deputy, Agent O'Neill, and I could all hear the colonel. The colonel was introduced to everyone listening. He then reviewed all eight of his reports on Selena Rodriquez. During this conversation we learned about the number of crimes Selena was suspected of committing over the past decade. In addition, we learned that her husband was possibly involved in several of her embezzlement/white collar crimes. Her husband was now on the run with numerous international arrest warrants issued by the National Police Corps. After a thirty-minute debriefing on these crimes, the colonel asked the group if anyone had any questions. The sheriff asked the colonel if he had any leads on where Selena's husband may have gone. He also asked if the colonel or anyone involved in Selena's investigations had made any connection to Maria Hernandez or Juan Lopez. The colonel stated that both names were found during the investigation in connection with several embezzlement crimes. He also said that both people appeared to be coordinating a group of individuals running a criminal organization. The colonel added that this latter bit of information was recently found about four weeks earlier when one of his detectives found an email sent to both Maria and Juan having something to do with a treasure ship and drugs. The sheriff then asked his detectives if anyone had any more questions for the colonel. No one did, except for me.

"Colonel, have any of your detectives looking into this case speculated where any of these three suspects may have gone?" I asked. There was some muffled conversation in Spanish; then the colonel stated, "One of my female detectives, Officer Cavallero, has suggested that our department find those countries that have a climate similar to Seville, where Selena may have lived with her husband some time ago." The Colonel then asked us if we had any additional information. Agent O'Neill asked who would be coordinating the investigations between Spain and the U.S. here at the sheriff's department. The colonel stated that he was the primary investigator handling any type of international cooperation between our countries. There were no further questions, so Sgt. Doaks asked if he could contact the colonel in a few days to update his department with any new information the sheriff's department had generated. The Colonel said yes, then hung up.

The sheriff and the Chief Deputy left the area, leaving Doaks, Agent O'Neill, and me. Nobody said anything for a very awkward minute or two; then Doaks said, "Well, s - -t."

Agent O'Neill added, "Can we all just agree to share any information we get with each other?"

"Fine with us," Doaks stated, looking at me. I agreed. As I began to leave the area, Doaks said, "Rookie, where do you think you are going?"

I glared at him and said, "I am going to the restroom. Is that ok?" Then I left. Doaks shook his head and then told O'Neill that I was going to drive him nuts. O'Neill just stood there with his left hand covering the smile on his face thinking, *This is going to be an interesting time with these two!*

Later, Doaks came into my office and apologized for his actions. I told him thanks; then he left. I wondered whether Doaks was getting some type of conscience. I again hit the pin icon for this day on my phone calendar, thinking Doaks must be starting to like me—NOT!

At 2:00 p.m. I was called into the sheriff's conference room with Sgt. Doaks and Agent O'Neill. Inside the conference room were a number of other police officers I did not know except for one: Clutch. Clutch, also known as Charles Thomas Hudson, was the assistant director of our state's DPS criminal investigations division. Doaks came over to me and whispered, "We got a lot of brass here!" Clutch saw me and was about to come over, but he was interrupted by the sheriff. We were all told to take our seats.

The sheriff began to brief us on why he had called all of us together. Over the next fifteen minutes, the sheriff introduced a newly formed international task force. There were seven individuals named to the task force, and each one was introduced by the sheriff. First, Colonel Ortez, Director of the National Police in Spain, then Agent O'Neill, FBI special agent whose expertise was international investigations and extradition. He continued with Assistant Director Hudson, head of the Florida Department of Public Safety Criminal Investigations Division; Agent Burns, DPS investigator expert in forensics, Lt. Lincoln (PhD), expert criminal psychologist; and Sgt. Doaks and Detective Hood, homicide division of the Mangrove County Sheriff's Department. The sheriff then asked Assistant DPS Director Hudson to lead the group in the United States while Colonel Ortez would lead a similar group in Spain. The sheriff requested that the group continue meeting to provide him with five major objectives that would focus on finding and extraditing Maria Hernandez and anyone associated with her in the past. After this charge was given, the sheriff left the room.

Doaks looked at me and shook his head. "Crap," he snorted. "Why am I on this fiasco, and why are you on it too?" I was just about to answer when Clutch got everyone's attention.

"Before we get started, I would like each of us to take five minutes to introduce ourselves and let everyone know a little about each of us, including where we work and what our field of expertise is. Then give me *two objectives* you believe would be critical to our mission in finding Hernandez and her associates." He was just about to sit down when he called on me. "Detective Hood, would you and Sgt. Doaks go first? Please introduce yourselves; then give our group a synopsis of your investigation into Maria Hernandez to date."

I stood up and looked at Doaks, who was kicking me under the table mouthing for me to sit down. I ignored him, took a deep breath, and spoke. For the next twenty minutes, I briefed the task force members on all of the actions Sgt. Doaks and I had been involved in regarding the investigation of several homicides over the past month. I told the task force members we believed that Maria Hernandez was directly or indirectly involved in all of these.

Once I was finished, Doaks nodded his head and whispered, "Great job, Rookie!" I sat down.

For the next thirty minutes, each member of the task force introduced themselves, including their areas of expertise, then gave Clutch several suggestions for objectives. Doaks and I sat there and listened. After everyone had made their introductions, Clutch asked Sgt. Doaks to tell the task force his suggestions. Doaks stood up, looked around the room, then reviewed everyone's suggestions. He then winked at me and said, "First, I believe everyone on this task force—federal, state, and local cops—needs to understand that all information from our investigations must be shared equally without any one area claiming success. Rank or government entity has no matter in this process." Doaks then asked each member of the task force to nod their head in agreement to his first objective. All members did. Then he continued, suggesting that our next objective should be to conduct an extensive background investigation on Commander Juan Lopez and Dispatcher Supervisor Jose James. Each of these men had assisted Maria Hernandez in numerous ways over the past decade or longer. Each man could have had something in their backgrounds, in their residences, or in their bank accounts that might give us a clue to a possible location where Lopez and Hernandez had fled. Doaks then sat down, looked at me, and smiled.

Clutch stood and asked everyone for their opinions on having the task force do an in-depth internal affairs (IA) investigation. Agent O'Neill stood and asked Doaks and me if our IA section would be able to conduct this in-depth investigation while the task force could focus on other areas. Doaks stated, "Yes." He felt our IA unit would have the best chance of investigating both moles in the sheriff's department. The task force members agreed with Agent O'Neill, and he sat down.

Doaks stood and told the task force that he would advise the sheriff on our IA recommendations on Lopez and James. Clutch then went to a large whiteboard in the room and wrote the number one priority of our task force:

FIND MARIA HERNANDEZ AND JUAN LOPEZ.

Chapter Five:

Catching a Break

September 16, 2021

It had been three weeks since the search warrants were executed at Maria Hernandez's residences. Three weeks and we had nothing—*nothing*—to move on. "Crud, crud, and crud," I sighed to myself.

Doaks came over to my office and said, "We need to catch a break on something. What are we missing?" I was just sitting there looking up, silently asking the Good Lord for something—*something*—we could jump on to get going on this investigation. I was just about to get some coffee when Clutch and O'Neill appeared.

"Hood, I need to pick your brain on something."

"OK, what?" I asked.

"If you were Maria Hernandez, given all of the information you know about her, where in the world would you go and disappear?" he asked. That question stopped me cold.

Frantically, my brain kicked into overdrive, thinking, *Where would Maria go?* I looked over at Doaks, who was standing with his jaw dropped toward the floor, then smiled.

"I would go to a location where the climate was similar to the Keys and where there was enough potential criminal activity that I could start my own criminal organization!" I exclaimed.

Clutch then clapped his hands, as did Doaks, and the new federal guy O'Neill nodded his head in agreement. *Look at them*, I thought. *They remind me of the Three Musketeers or the Three Stooges, depending on their actions during the day!*

"Great idea, Hood," O'Neill said. Doaks was rubbing his balding head, and Clutch was still smiling.

"Hood, you have some great insights into human behavior. Let's start with your idea and get the task force working on your two elements: climate and crime." Clutch left, O'Neill followed, and Doaks was still scratching his head when he came over to my desk and sat down.

"Rookie, why didn't I think of that?" he asked. I thought, *Because you need to refresh your mind and get into using the internet for answers*, but I didn't say anything. Doaks then looked at me and asked, "Do you have any other brilliant ideas on finding Hernandez?"

"Yes, I have at least one more I didn't mention: non-extradition countries." "Nonextradition countries! What the heck are you talking about?"

I explained to Doaks what a non-extradition country

meant to a criminal. It meant that a criminal wanted for multiple crimes, with a keen sense of forming a criminal organization with a significant amount of hands-on cash, could live in that country and *not* be extradited back to the United States. These things were exactly what Maria was looking for outside of our country. I believed that we needed to focus our resources on these areas, and then we needed a break in our investigation.

Doaks left, still scratching his head. I started my own research on climate and non-extradition countries. I started with Google and found that there were many countries with non-extradition treaties involving the United States. Once I counted about 80 countries, I sat down and reviewed this list. I thought to myself that there were a lot of countries that do *not* want the United States coming onto their soil to arrest criminals. *Crud, this is a long list. Now what types of climate do some of these countries have, and which ones best match the climate of the Florida Keys?* Looking at the list again, I began to understand how big our world was and how many countries were located in the same longitude and latitude as the Keys. I started my search looking at the latitudes and longitudes for the Keys. I then took a globe and marked those countries inside the same latitudes and longitudes of the Keys. The list of countries was long.

I was just about to start another list when Doaks burst into my office, panting and out of breath. He yelled, "Rookie, we caught our first break! Key West PD found Lopez's POV (privately owned vehicle) in the basement garage of the Key West Marriott Beachside Hotel. It was buried under a pile of boxes and wooden pallets." Doaks then collapsed into my office chair and started sucking a lot of air. I ran over and gave him a high five, then started out the door toward my car.

"Wait! Wait, Rookie!" Doaks yelled. "We have to tell the task force about this finding." *Crap*, I thought to myself, *why didn't Doaks let the task force know?*

Doaks then explained that he had just received a call from his friend, the sergeant of homicide in the Key West PD. The sergeant stated that one of his officers discovered the car hidden under a pile of junk, ran the VIN (vehicle identification number), got a hit, then contacted his sergeant. That sergeant then contacted Doaks.

He was really sucking in air now. I returned to my office and asked Doaks if he was going to live. He gestured a finger at me, then slowly rose from his seat. "Look," Doaks muttered, "We have to bring in the task force on this one. We have to play by the rules, share everything with everyone!" I nodded my head and agreed; then we both headed into the area assigned to our task force.

Doaks and I walked into the task force conference room. Clutch was there and asked me what we found. Doaks answered in a loud voice, "We caught our first break. Lopez's POV has been found in a Key West hotel." Everyone stopped what they were doing, and Clutch asked Doaks to please repeat this great news. Doaks did, and Clutch said, "OK,

Doaks, you and Hood go—Burns, you too—and have the
new forensic nurse meet you there. And take the crime kit."
Clutch looked around the room. "Anyone else want to go?"
No one responded, so off we went.

Doaks drove his car, while I drove my patrol vehicle to
the hotel. Burns and his new forensic nurse (*Who the heck is
this?* I thought) arrived in separate cars. The local police did a
great job in isolating the vehicle. They had frozen the scene and
did nothing as far as processing the scene until we all arrived.
Doaks and I were out of the car, heading toward the suspect's
vehicle, when this new person beat us to the car location. She
must be the forensic nurse. Her name was Colleen Laszacko.
She was gloved up with mask, booties, hair net, and a one-
piece Tyvek investigative suit. She was all business, and she
was heading straight toward the car.

Doaks yelled at her: "Stop! Do not go near this car!" She
turned, looked at Burns, then Doaks, then me.

"Why not?" she snorted.

"Possible IEDs," Doaks stated. He then told all of us to
back up and wait. He had contacted the local bomb squad to
do a thorough check of the vehicle prior to anyone touching
anything on this car. *What the heck is Doaks thinking?* I asked
myself, but he reminded me how many IEDs were found in
the escape passageway at Maria's penthouse.

We all stepped back when the bomb techs arrived to let
them and their robot, C-4, check out the vehicle. Two hours
later, one IED was found. It was set to explode once any car

door was opened. The IED was defused, and the car was checked again by a bomb dog. The dog did not alert on any section of the car. Doaks then turned to this new forensic nurse, Laszacko, and said, "OK, go for it, but know that I am watching everything you do."

Laszacko thanked Doaks and started processing the car.

Burns looked at Doaks and said, "You have no idea who you're dealing with. She is the best forensic nurse in the country, and she will eat your lunch—so cool it before she tears your head off!" Dang, I love watching Doaks get taken down, but I was very impressed by this forensic nurse and continued to watch her work.

Doaks and I have a lot of forensic tools and investigative equipment to use at our sheriff's department, but Laszacko was bringing out tools I had only seen in evidence or forensic magazines. Within twenty minutes, she had sprayed some type of liquid on all of the doors, the door handles, the inside windows, and all inside locking devices, cup holders, and air vents. Next she was spraying another mixture on the seats, the seat belts, and the seat belt buckles. Then she opened a case and pulled out a lightweight, forensic-designed vacuum and began to vacuum everything in the vehicle. While Laszacko was doing her work, I went over to her location inside the car and asked her if there was something I could do to help her. She looked up, sweating like a racehorse, and told me, "No, but thanks." She then went back to her job.

Doaks looked at Burns and asked, "What is with this

woman? Does she not believe in teamwork?" Burns laughed at Doaks' question and said, "Colleen can get more evidence using these new DNA and fingerprint sprays in about five minutes than you and Hood and a team of expert crime scene investigators could get in ten hours. She will find and collect any evidence in one-tenth the time, and she will have all of the evidence including DNA evidence identified, photographed, and processed in one hour. You all would have taken hours—if not days—to process this car. So be quiet and watch her work, but be prepared when she calls you to jump. She takes no orders and shoves people around, but she is the best."

Once she was finished inside and outside the car, she opened the hood. There she began taking out the air filters and any other air cleaning devices she found. In addition, she pulled out the cabin filters inside the car and placed everything into cardboard boxes marked "Evidence." Finally, any debris left inside the tire treads or inside the wheel wells was collected and put into more evidence boxes. Just when we thought she was done, she called me over to her location inside the driver's side of the car. There she asked, "Detective Hood, would you please take out your pen light and look around the driver's seat belt buckle?"

"Sure," I told her and began to look all around the seat belt buckle. I didn't see anything at first; then she told me to look inside the buckle, where the seat belt buckles into the holder. I did, and there it was: something small—very small—lying against the holder of the seat belt tongue. Laszacko handed me a set of unusual tweezers, about twelve inches long and very slim. I took these hyper-tough fine-point tweezers and inserted them into the buckle. After looking into the buckle where the seat belt tongue is located, I pulled out a small piece of paper. I held it in the tweezers and gave it to Laszacko, who put it into an evidence bag. "How did you notice that piece of evidence?" I asked her.

"Special glasses," she said, producing high-magnifying glasses that had two small lights on each side and emitted an incredible amount of light. *Dang*, I thought, *I need a pair of these*. But I just stood there and watched her wrap things up.

Doaks then asked Burns if he had asked the on-duty patrol sergeant if anyone had done a search of all of the trash containers in the area. Burns said that he had not, then told Doaks to go ahead and ask the on-duty sergeant and several of his officers to look in all of the trash containers in the garage. Burns also told the sergeant to have some additional officers look in the pool area. Five minutes later, one of the patrol officers yelled for Doaks or me to come to his location in the garage. I got there and looked into the trash can. There, buried under some old food paper plates, were two containers of Septic Shock. I photographed these containers, then got two large evidence bags and put both containers in them. Next, Laszacko came over and told me to open the bags. I did, and she sprayed something that covered the entire containers. Within seconds, there appeared several smudged fingerprints or palm prints. Laszacko then produced a small camera, photographed the prints, and hit the "Send" button on her camera.

"What the heck kind of camera is that?" I asked.

"A very special one," she stated, took the evidence from me, and put it into the back of her truck. *Dang, I need to work more with this woman because she has some incredible forensic tools.*

Doaks and Burns came over to my location and stated that they had found no other evidence in the area. Doaks looked at me and asked, "Why were those two containers evidence?" I told him that the containers had contents that could destroy blood and DNA.

"Blood and DNA evidence?" he asked.

"Yes. I have been studying ways to destroy crime scene evidence over the past month, and that bottle brand, called "Septic Shock," will destroy any blood or DNA evidence left at a crime scene.

"Crap," Doaks muttered to himself. "I need to start researching some of these things too."

"What did you just say?" I asked.

"Nothing, Rookie. Let's head back to Marathon."

Chapter Six:

Hunting for the Isabella

September 17–20, 2021

Today I began daydreaming about what I was doing with my family about one month ago. On that day my dad, my brothers, and I were diving off the shoreline of the Hut at a place called the Rockpile. After we caught our limit of lobsters, we found some interesting coins while we were diving. The coins were in good condition, so my dad hired an expert to clean them and determine their value. He also decided to begin researching the type of coins we found. Initially he was surprised to find that these coins were not too badly damaged by the salt water. He thought perhaps the canvas type of lining inside the little coin box we found might have protected them over the past 300 years. Dad's research indicated that these coins may be some form of Spanish money. If the coins contain silver, they are called an 8 reales. He also learned that these coins could be combined with gold in a variety of sizes. Their size could range from ½ to 1, 2, 4, and 8 reales. The value of each of these coins would vary depending on the age and the amount of gold and silver in them. Dad was waiting for the report from the coin expert to see how valuable these coins were given their age, condition, and gold content.

Also during this past month, my dad had begun researching stories of sunken ships located around Key Marathon. He found one ship, called the *Nuestra de Isabella*, that may have sunk on the Atlantic side of Key Marathon. He researched this ship and found that it was sailing from Havana, Cuba to Barcelona, Spain in June 1733. The ship was on a secret mission mandated by the King of Spain to secure his treasury from his wife, the queen. The ship left Havana in late June 1733 and was sailing north along the Keys when a hurricane struck. The ship was lost at sea. However, two months later, another ship sailing along the Keys picked up two sailors from an island. These men told the ship's captain that they were sailors on the *Isabella*. They said they had been shipwrecked on this island for at least two months. They were taken on board this ship and returned to Havana. In Cuba, the sailors related their survival story to an aide to the governor, who then contacted the governor of Havana. The governor was aware of the *Isabella's* secret mission and, after hearing the story, immediately launched a recovery effort to locate the ship. These sailors were part of this recovery mission and returned to the island where they were shipwrecked. The sailors told the captain the location off the island where they believed the *Isabella* sank. Numerous men attempted to dive in the location, but nothing was found. This recovery effort lasted for two weeks in this one location. Then another storm hit. The captain left the area and returned to Havana without any recovered items.

Following this failure, the governor was even more determined to find the *Isabella* and ordered one more recovery effort. This time the same surviving sailors from the *Isabella* accompanied this second recovery ship to the area they had searched during the first recovery effort. Again, after several weeks of hunting and diving in this location, nothing was found. And again, this captain—facing another tropical storm—left the area and sailed back to Havana without any recovered items. No other attempts at finding the *Isabella* occurred.

Shane Moldune and his new wife, Allie, arrived at the Key West International Airport on Saturday morning, September 18. My mom and dad met them at the baggage claim, then headed up to their condo in Key Marathon. Shane and Allie had planned this trip to enjoy the Keys. Shane also wanted to help his uncle attempt to follow a possible course where the sunken Spanish ship called the *Isabella* may have moved over the past 300 years in the Atlantic Ocean. Shane was a marine engineer who, after some questions from his cousin, Detective Katie Hood, and his Uncle Todd, had developed a new hydrodynamic theory. His theory involved studying this area to determine the impact of hurricanes on the islands in the Florida Keys. Shane's interest began once Todd and Katie asked him if he could research any theories on how to project the possible location where sunken ship(s) may have traveled in a 300-year period. This question piqued his interest and, as a result, he developed a theory. He then had it researched, tested, and validated by a number of other marine engineers. Now he was anxious to test his theory by helping my dad trace the possible location of the *Isabella* now. Weeks prior to Shane's arrival in Key West, my dad and Shane had discussed their plan. As a result, dad was going to rent an underwater drone to see if he and Shane could locate some materials or debris left by the *Isabella* using Shane's theory.

On Saturday night, I came over to mom and dad's condo to meet Shane and Allie for a lobster dinner. We reminisced about that day when my dad, my brothers, and I were diving when we found the coins. Dad had already showed Shane and Allie a few of these coins, and both were impressed by the quality of each coin.

Shane asked dad, "Why do you think each of these coins were in such good condition, showing little to no damage by the salt water?" Dad then showed Shane a piece of canvas lining he had taken out of the coin box the coins were in. Shane looked at the fabric, amazed to see how the canvas had protected these coins. For the rest of the evening, Shane, Allie, and my family caught up on family weddings, deaths, and new babies.

The next day, September 19, my dad had arranged to pick up the underwater drone in Key West. The minimum rental period was three days at $200 per day. This drone was the only deep-water drone equipped with side scanning radar, a camera, and an attached arm and was available only in Key West. It was called a "Geneinno Drone T1" and had a depth of 150 meters or 492 feet. Shane explained to me why he and dad had rented this drone. Given the possible starting point where the *Isabella* sank, he believed that the drone could follow a trail of debris left by the *Isabella*. Shane also explained his hydrodynamic theory, describing how a hurricane occurring above the water, over islands, can generate underwater tornadoes formed by eddies surrounding the islands in the Keys. He believed that given the depth of the water, the strength of the hurricane, and the weight of the sunken ship, he could determine the probable direction this ship could have traveled. Based on his formula, Shane believed that the *Isabella* had probably travelled ten to forty miles or more over the past 300 years. He also believed—based on the approximate tonnage of this ship, plus the depth of the water and the strength of these hurricanes—that he could project the path and possible location of this ship now. He told me how he created his underwater theory by using a model ship in a test drum. Inside this marine lab, he created an island, a sunken ship, varying depths of water, lots of sand, and a wind machine. Shane had researched hurricanes in the Keys and found that there were approximately fifty Category 3–5 hurricanes that had struck the Keys in the past 300 years. Given the projected strength of each hurricane, then looking at the impacts of each hurricane on the ocean floor and the weight of the *Isabella*, his theory resulted in him plotting a southeasterly to easterly path where he believed the Isabella may have moved. Given the depth of the ocean in this possible location, the drone had to be able to reach a projected depth of 490 to 500 feet. The drone they rented was the only underwater drone available that could go to the maximum depth to see if any additional debris could be located from the *Isabella*.

After listening to Shane explain his theory, I was excited to see how his project would end. The coins we found appeared to be from the same century when the *Isabella* sank. Dad and Shane were hoping to find some more coins, jewelry, or other items they could use to determine if the *Isabella* had been driven along this projected pathway.

Shane and dad picked up the underwater drone in Key West, attached it to the car with a specially designed carrier, and headed back to Marathon. They got the drone onto dad's boat, then headed to the south side of Marathon. They began their search there, first by putting the drone into the water about one-half mile offshore from the Hut. Then they went through a test dive working all of the controls making sure that the radar, the camera, and the arm worked. Once the drone had successfully passed this initial dive, Shane and dad set a southeastern course following Shane's projections. They had gone about five or six miles into the Atlantic when the drone radar and camera picked up something at a depth of 200 feet. The object appeared to be a lump of something.

Shane studied the camera and the radar soundings and told Todd to hold the boat in this position. Shane then activated the drone's arm and attempted to lift the object. The object did not move immediately. It took a lot of shaking; then slowly the object moved, and eventually the arm secured it. Slowly the drone ascended. Within ten minutes the drone appeared to be near the surface, dragging the object on one side. Shane maneuvered the drone to the boat and roped the object in the drone's arm. The object was then brought onto the boat and immediately put into the bait holding box. The lump was covered in sand and barnacles. It looked like one long piece of metal attached to a clump of other things. Both Todd and Shane tried to figure out what they had pulled from this location but did not know what they had just brought on board. Since it was evening, they took the drone out of the water, placed it into the boat, and headed home.

Once home they secured the drone inside the storage shed. Then they took the object they found from the bait box on the boat, placed it into a large cooler filled with salt water, and brought it onto the patio. After showing their wives their find, both men set the object in the salt water. Todd told Shane that the best thing they could do now was to let the object sit in the salt water while he contacted his coin expert, Sam Burton.

Burton was a local expert and a member of the American Numismatic Association whose specialty was salvaging old coins from sunken ships. Todd had contacted Burton to clean up and evaluate the coins he and Katie had found a few weeks ago. Burton told Todd that if he found any more coins or metal objects, he should keep them in salt water and bring them to him as soon as possible. Todd had agreed to take whatever he and Shane found to Burton.

Todd contacted Burton that night, and at 8:00 a.m. the next day the object inside the cooler was delivered to him. Todd explained to Shane that cleaning the object they just found would probably take months. According to Burton, the object needed time in distilled water to begin the cleaning process. Burton said he would clean the object with a toothbrush each week, replacing the distilled water for months if necessary. If this process did not work after two months, he would then clean the object with pure olive oil. The cleaning process would occur for a week in the olive oil, changing the oil after each daily cleaning session. If that did not work, he would use electrolysis. This process would be difficult to regulate but, after getting the right amount of electricity, the object could become clean or recognizable in about twenty to thirty minutes. Todd told Shane that this process would be expensive; Shane agreed to help pay his share.

By 10:00 a.m. the next day, Shane and dad were back in the Atlantic. They were about eight miles out when they submerged the drone and started heading southeast for another mile. At about 11:30 a.m., the drone's sonar picked up a large metal object partially buried on the ocean floor. Shane studied the sonar image and told Todd to hold the boat steady over the object. Shane then used the drone's propellers to clear away the sand and silt around the object. As the object became clearer, Shane let out a gasp. "I think we just found a torpedo; in fact, I think this may be a World War II torpedo!"

Todd let Shane control the boat, and he too looked at the sonar and then the drone's camera indicating an object that looked like a torpedo. "Holy crap," Todd exclaimed. "I think you are right!" The object they had just found appeared to be over twenty feet long, had the diameter of a large barrel, and had some markings on it. It was down about 250 feet. At this depth Shane had a hard time focusing the camera and lights on the markings, so he took several pictures on his cell phone.

Todd asked Shane, "Have you taken any type of ordnance training in your Navy in-service schools?"

Shane replied, "Yes, I just had a course titled 'Ordnance Power and Propulsion.' In fact, the instructor of the course, Retired Sergeant Major Steven Bourne, and I developed a friendship during the course. I have his phone number, and I believe he would know immediately what type of torpedo this is. He has a hobby of studying World War II ordnances. If I can get any cell phone reception out here, I could call him and send a picture."

Todd told Shane that the cell bars out this far offshore are nil. He said, "Let's mark this location on my fish finder, then head in closer to Duck Key to get some reception." They marked the location, then headed to Duck Key. There Shane was able to contact Bourne and sent him a few pictures of the torpedo.

Shane asked Todd, "Can we stay here and grab some lunch? Bourne said he could get back to me in twenty minutes."

"Sure," Todd said. "Let's dock the boat here. There is a great seafood restaurant on the other side of the dock." Todd was getting out of the boat when Shane told him, "Get my food to go. One of us has to stay here with this drone."

"Of course," Todd said. "I will get both orders to go."

Todd returned, and they both ate fish sandwiches. Shane's phone rang. On the phone was a very excited Bourne. Shane put the phone on speaker, and they both listened as Bourne explained that he believed the cell phone picture may be a World War II German torpedo, probably a T II class, called a "WREN." He also stated that Shane needed to contact the Navy to get an underwater demolition dive team down at the site.

"Why?" Shane asked.

Bourne replied, "To defuse any potential explosives and to retrieve the torpedo for additional research." He then asked Shane to take as many pictures as possible and send them to him before the torpedo was brought to the surface. Bourne also asked if Shane knew any admirals to contact to get a dive team to respond. Shane told Bourne that he knew the right person to contact, then hung up the phone.

"Wow, this is nuts," Todd said. "How does a World War II German torpedo end up at this location?"

Shane, still on the boat in Duck Key, pulled up his phone contacts and found a number listed under R. E. Lee. After a few rings—and a few receptionists—Shane began talking to Rear Admiral R. E. Lee. Lee listened to the description of the torpedo and the tentative findings by Bourne.

The Admiral said, "Bourne is an expert on this type of find. So if he says we need to get a dive team there, I will order one to meet you at the Coast Guard Station on Key Marathon as soon as possible. Do you have the location marked?"

"Yes," Shane told the admiral, "I believe it would be in the best interest of the Navy to have a Coast Guard ship on that site to secure the scene until the dive team arrives." The Admiral thanked Shane and hung up.

"It is very unusual to find a torpedo—specifically one that appears to be a German torpedo—in this area," Todd stated. Shane agreed, then received a call from the local Coast Guard commander, Captain Kirk. Shane answered his phone and put it on speaker. The captain asked if Shane could meet his ship at the site of the torpedo location. Shane answered yes and gave the captain the coordinates. After the call, Todd filled the boat with gas and took off toward the location of this torpedo.

At 3:30 p.m. Shane and Todd were at the site of the suspected torpedo. The Coast Guard ship arrived at 4:00 p.m. An officer called over to Todd's boat, identified himself as Lieutenant Junior Grade Smart, and asked to come aboard. Todd brought the boat close to the Coast Guard ship, and Smart came on board. After everyone was introduced, the lieutenant asked to see the pictures Shane and Todd had taken of the object. Then Smart asked if it were possible to place the drone into the water, submersed in the location, so that he could view the object. Shane agreed and launched the drone. Fifteen minutes later, the drone was hovering over the object, and Smart began videotaping. He used a unique shaped camera and, once he was done, had his ship brought over. He thanked us and asked if we could retrieve the drone and head over to the Coast Guard station to meet the dive team leader. "Sure," Todd said. They retrieved the drone and headed to the Coast Guard station.

Chapter Seven:
Uncovering More Mysteries

September 18, 2021

At 7:30 p.m. at the Coast Guard base on Marathon, the U.S. Navy Demolition Deep Sea Dive Team arrived. The supervisor, having the rank of sergeant, came over to greet Todd and Shane. The sergeant asked them if they had any pictures of the object they just located. Shane said that they did and showed him the video from the drone camera. The sergeant said, "Thanks, we will take if from here," then left.

Shane asked the sergeant if they could come along to watch the recovery efforts. "No," he replied. "If this torpedo is still functional after all these years, we have to disarm it first, then bring it to the surface. All of this will take between four and six hours."

After he left, Todd and Shane returned to the condo and discussed these events with my mom and my cousin-in-law. I came over for dinner, got filled in by Shane and dad on what they found, and wondered why a WWII German torpedo would be found in this area.

Earlier that day

Doaks called me at 7:00 a.m. Saturday morning. "Hood, are you up?"

"No! Why are you calling me on my usual day off?" I asked.

"The sheriff just advised me that the ground penetrating radar unit you requested arrived at headquarters (HQ) five minutes ago. He wants us down there ASAP," Doaks ordered.

Nuts, I thought. *Why is that unit here now? It was delayed until next Friday.* "OK, I will meet you at HQ in fifteen minutes," I said and hung up.

I met Doaks at HQ at 7:45 a.m. Then we met Sgt. Duce, who introduced himself and asked if we would like to see a demonstration of how this new unit worked. "Sure," we said and headed outside the department to where the GPR (ground penetrating radar) unit was set up. Duce went over some of the basic operations of his machine as he was preparing its use. This model was a GP Rover. Duce explained that he knew about some items buried in the grass. He wanted to show us how these objects appeared on the GPR screen. Duce then brought both of us over to the machine, got it operational, and began to move the device along the ground. There was nothing in the first minute, but soon an object appeared. Duce held the device over the object, adjusted some dials, and let us look. There on the screen was a large pipe. Duce said that this was the water line into our department. He held the device in place and adjusted some buttons, and a very clear image of the water line became visible. Next he adjusted another button, and the depth of the radar went down five feet. Again Doaks and I were impressed by how this machine worked. Duce then took the machine a little further, then stopped. Here he showed us the gas pipe running into our station. The gas pipe was down about five to six feet, and again Duce adjusted his dials so the pipe location was readily seen. He then described how he would be using the GPR to detect any human remains. He stated that if any bodies were found at the crime scene, he hoped they would be wrapped in some type of covering because the wrapping materials would make them easier to detect. He continued explaining how comparing GPR imagery using between 500 MHz and 250 MHz antenna would provide the best pictures if a body was buried.

He then showed us another device called an EMI (electromagnetic induction meter), which helps locate unmarked graves. Duce concluded his demonstration by telling us the amount of training he had received. He told us that this device could locate bodies, but research was still ongoing for ways to increase its efficiency.

His next question was tough for us to answer. "Is there any water near the crime scene where we are going?" I looked at Doaks and rolled my eyes, thinking, *We're on an island, so obviously there is water nearby. How is this going to work?*

Doaks and I shook our heads, then turned to Duce. "Do you think your GPR could work in the sand adjacent to the ocean?" we asked.

Duce did not answer our question right away. He rubbed his chin and asked, "How close is the ocean?" I told him approximately ten feet away if the tide was not coming in. Duce said nothing. He left and went back to his vehicle, pulled out a large manual, and began reading. Doaks and I headed back to our patrol unit and waited.

Duce approached and asked, "How big is the crime scene area, and how far away from the ocean?" Doaks and I looked at each other.

"The crime scene itself appears to be about ten feet long by five feet wide. We had a cadaver dog alert on two positions inside this area. We uncovered three bodies in one location. We were asking for a GPR unit to look in the area," I said.

Duce shook his head. "We need to go to the scene. Let me look at the area. Then I can decide whether I can use the device or not."

"OK," I said, then told him to pack up his machine and follow us to the crime scene.

Doaks and I arrived at the Hut at the same time. We exited our vehicles and waited for Duce. He arrived, and we all walked to the crime scene. Over the past month, nothing much had changed. The scene was protected with crime scene tape. The holes I had dug to locate the bodies were filled with sand, and the beach was empty.

Duce asked me, "Can you show me exactly where you found your bodies?"

"Sure," I said as I walked over to the sunken areas in the sand and pointed out the locations.

"Where did the cadaver dog sit down?" he asked.

I moved over about three feet adjacent to the concrete seawall. "Here," I pointed.

Doaks looked at me and asked, "How do you know exactly where that dog sat down?" I showed him a photograph I took while Mutt, the cadaver dog, was sitting down along the seawall. "Nice job, Rookie," he whispered. I wanted to kick him but didn't.

Duce began to walk a grid pattern over the crime scene. He looked at the wall, the sand, and the ocean. He asked me, "While you were digging up these bodies, did you have any problem with water?"

"No," I stated, "not at first. However, when the tide came in, we had to block the water from entering these gravesites using a sand barrier."

"Sand barrier?" Duce asked.

"Yes, we borrowed a small tractor with a scoop shovel from the construction site across the street. The barrier worked until we cleared the crime scene later that night."

"Interesting approach," Duce stated. Doaks told him we were always thinking ahead. *Right*, I thought.

Duce went back to his car and returned with his manual.

"I think I would like to try my GPR out on this crime scene, but I need to know if we can create another sand barrier in the area. I am worried about the water coming into the area while I am trying to run the GPR," Duce stated. I looked at Doaks, then left the scene. I went across the street and found the construction site closed, but there was an emergency number listed. I called and talked to the foreman who said that he would come down, unlock the site, and drive his tractor over to the scene. I thanked him and returned to the scene.

"I just contacted the foreman of the construction site across the street, and he agreed to open the site and drive the tractor over here to assist us," I told Duce and Doaks.

By 11:30 a.m., with the help of the foreman, the crime scene had a ten-foot-long, three-foot-high barrier of sand located five feet south of the crime scene. Duce made a grid, stepped off his outside boundaries, got his machine operational, and started his grid pattern. He was about five minutes into the grid pattern when he stopped. He looked closer at the screen, adjusted a few buttons, then found a body.

He called me over. "Look at this," he said.

"Wow!" I paused. "That is yet another body."

"Where is Doaks?" Duce asked.

"He's in the restroom. He will be out in a few minutes," I told him.

Five minutes later, Doaks came over and asked, "Did we find anything yet?" Duce confirmed that we had one body located down somewhere between four and six feet. "No, s - -t," Doaks croaked.

Duce continued, "I have one body, but I would like to continue on my grid to see if there might be another body buried in the same area." He resumed working his grid, and two minutes later he stopped. He adjusted his screen, contrasted his gain button, then exclaimed, "I have another body here!" *Crud, crud, and more crud*, I thought. I looked at Doaks, who was on his phone with the sheriff, asking for more manpower and body bags.

I went over to Duce and looked at his screen. There, again, was another body. "How deep is this one compared to the other body?" I asked. Duce adjusted some more dials, looked at one of his tracking devices, then said, "The last body is very deep; my guess is about ten to fifteen feet or more. I believe it has been here for a long period of time, and it appears to be wrapped in some type of object. I have only seen this type of situation in my classroom training. I think this body may be several decades old if not more," he stated.

Since both bodies were located several feet down, hand-digging them out would be difficult. I called my friend Clutch to get his advice.

"Hood, for Pete's sake, it is Saturday morning and my only day off. Why are you bothering me now?" he asked.

"Clutch, I need your help. I need to pick your brain on how to recover two bodies, each buried in the sand, here at the Hut. One body is four to six feet down; the other is closer to ten feet. What are your recommendations on digging up both?" I asked.

"Wait, you're telling me there are two more bodies near the original crime scene at the Hut?" he asked.

"Yes," I reiterated.

"How did you locate these bodies on a Saturday?" he asked. I told him about Duce, the ground penetrating radar unit, and the results. Clutch didn't say a thing for a minute, then told me, "Please put Sgt. Duce on the phone." For the next five minutes, Duce and Clutch talked. I didn't understand a lot of what they were talking about, but I did decipher that some of the conversation involved the depth of the bodies and the accuracy of the GPR. I heard their conversation ending; then Duce gave me back my phone.

"Hood," said Clutch, " I want you to follow Duce's instructions on removing these two bodies. I also want you to call Dr. Spock and get him there ASAP. I am very concerned that once these bodies hit the air, they may disintegrate."

"OK, how do we preserve these bodies in this environment?" I asked.

"I'm working on that. Jeez, give me a break, Hood," he said, then hung up.

Duce motioned me over to his location. "I think it would be a good idea to contact your district attorney. If these two bodies were in the adjacent area where you found the first three bodies, and at that location you had the pretense of a possible homicide scene, you could dig these bodies up and proceed with your investigation. However, these two bodies are not in the same location. They are adjacent to the original crime scene, so you need to get his legal opinion on whether we need a warrant before we begin to dig these people up." *Crud*, I thought again, *Duce is probably right.*

I agreed, took out my cell phone, and contacted Don Moceri, our district attorney.

"Hello, this is Moceri," he answered.

"Mr. Moceri, this is Detective Hood. I am sorry to disturb you on this Saturday morning, but I need your help. I am at the Hut, with Sgts. Doaks and Duce. Duce is a ground penetrating radar technician. We have just done a sweep of our original crime scene at the Hut. We just found two more bodies in an area a few feet away from the excavation site of the three bodies we exhumed last month. Do we have any legal grounds to remove these bodies today, or should we get a search warrant?"

"That is a great legal question," he said. "Let me do a few things, and I will meet you at the crime scene in thirty minutes." He hung up.

Doaks came over and asked, "What did you and Clutch talk about?" I told him we were discussing how to dig up these bodies without having them disintegrate. Then I told him I called Mr. Moceri. "What the heck, Hood, why are you calling Moceri on this?" Doaks asked.

"Because Duce and I were talking. Given his experience in these types of findings, he believes we need to talk to our district attorney prior to digging up these bodies since they are not located directly in the crime scene. And since these bodies appear to be old—in fact, one he believes may be hundreds of years old—Duce suggested I contact the district attorney," I explained.

"Well, crap," he said and walked off.

Duce watched Doaks stomp off and called me over again. "Hey, does he do that a lot?" he asked.

"Yes. When I hit one of his buttons and he knows I am right, he generally leaves the area and returns two minutes later to apologize," I said. Sure enough, Doaks came back, called me over, and apologized.

"You are right, Hood. I should have thought to call Moceri, but for some reason I didn't. I am sorry I jumped at you."

"Sarge, no problem. A lot of different things are happening here today, and we are a team. I don't want to jeopardize our homicide cases. We need to figure out what all this evidence points to," I said. I turned to Duce and had him come over to our location for an update. I started, "Moceri will be here in ten minutes. I believe we may have to get a search warrant to dig up these bodies. Duce, what do you have?"

Duce stated, "I believe you are doing the right thing in contacting your district attorney. We need to be sure that we have some legal rationale to dig up these two bodies buried I believe a long time ago."

"Doaks, what is your update?" I asked him.

He said, "The sheriff cannot believe we are finding more bodies in this same area. He has authorized more overtime and more personnel to guard this area until we conclude this investigation."

Just then my phone rang, and it was Clutch. "Hood, I have a solution to our bodies. We need to have Dr. Spock place both of them into a double body bag, partially filled with wet sand and some salt water."

"Clutch, wait—first I have our district attorney on his way to determine if we need to get a warrant to exhume these bodies."

"Why?" Clutch asked.

"Because they are not in the same crime scene as the other three bodies. They are adjacent to this scene," I told him.

"Crud, you are right on this one, Hood. And I hate it when you are right. How did you think this one up?" he asked.

"I didn't. Sgt. Duce did. Moceri is coming here and, once he is done, I'll call you back." I then hung up.

I love getting a few shots at Clutch just to keep him on his toes, I chuckled to myself.

Moceri showed up and walked over to our location. He introduced himself to Sgt. Duce, then asked to see the two bodies. After he and Duce talked for about five minutes, he came over to Doaks and me. "Hood, can you please show me the location of the three bodies you found about a month ago?" he asked.

"Yes," I said and walked over to the three shallow holes in the sand about five feet west of the seawall.

"Since these bodies are not buried in same location of

our three prior bodies, I am going to get a search warrant. I need the court's permission to dig up these two other bodies," Moceri told us. "Please give me another hour or so; then I will call you with the warrant to start the exhumation process," he said as he left.

Doaks and I looked at each other, then asked Duce, "Do you feel your depths on each of these bodies is pretty accurate?"

"Yes," he stated, "I believe we could use the backhoe on that tractor we borrowed. If the operator is skilled enough, we can exhume these two bodies in one hour or less, provided we get the warrant to exhume them." I left the area, then asked the foreman sitting on the tractor if he felt he was expert enough to dig close to each of the bodies.

He said, "I have operated a backhoe for twenty years, so I believe I can put this shovel on top of each of these bodies."

Given that information, I returned to Doaks and Duce and waited.

Chapter Eight:

Exhuming Bodies and More Discoveries

September 18, 2021: Later that day

At 2:30 p.m. Moceri called and told us to contact Dr. Spock and begin exhuming the bodies. I called Dr. Spock, told him we had the legal authority to exhume the two bodies, and asked if he could prepare the body bags. Dr. Spock stated that he was coming over with three double body bags, all prepared according to the best guesstimates of Clutch and himself. I went over to the foreman on the tractor and had him follow me to a location where he could maneuver his backhoe into a safe position to begin the exhumation process.

Thirty seconds into digging in the sand, the stabilizing bars on the backhoe sank. The foreman directed the three of us to go into the construction site and bring back three two-by-ten boards and four concrete blocks. Doaks balked at the request, but Duce and I continued and within two minutes had these things on site. The foreman showed us where to put the three two-by-ten boards and where to stack the four concrete blocks. Once these pieces were in place, we resumed the exhumation process. Within five minutes, the foreman stopped digging and told me to get into the hole. After I jumped in, I put my shovel in the sand two inches below his backhoe where I hit an object. I slowly began to clear away the sand. Doaks stopped me until he could create a sieve using several old lounge chairs in the area. He then told me to continue. I slowly began removing the sand around the object. Using the sieve, I put five more shovels of sand through it. Nothing was found. With the sixth shovel, I noticed an object sticking out of the sand in my shovel. I put the sand and the object through the sieve and found a wallet. All work stopped, and I began taking pictures.

In the meantime, Doaks recorded the exhumation process. He continued filming once I found the wallet. I quickly documented our evidence find, then continued slowly digging. I found a body on my next shovel. As Doaks continued filming, I slowly began clearing the sand from around the body. The body was wrapped in some type of canvas covering, which I initially thought was plastic. The tarp was covered in dried paint and wrapped the entire body. After I processed the homicide scene, photographed the area, and took measurements, I looked up and saw that Dr. Spock had arrived.

"Hood, are you ready for us to get the body out of the scene?" Spock asked.

"Yes, but let me verify with Sgt. Doaks." Doaks was nodding his head to go ahead while he continued filming. Then Spock's two assistants took my place in the hole, dragged the prepared body bag into it, carefully placed the body into the body bag, and closed the bag. They lifted the body out of the hole, placed it on a gurney, and waited.

I got back into the hole. I continued shoveling the sand and found another object. The object appeared to be the handle of a knife. I placed this shovel of sand into the sieve and found a large knife. Again, I stopped the process, documented the scene, measured the knife, and added it to the other evidence I had collected. *Crud*, I thought to myself. *What does all this evidence mean?* Then I looked up, prayed to God, and thanked Him for letting us find all this evidence on a body buried decades ago.

Duce told me to stop digging. He had me measure the depth of the hole. The hole was five feet deep, so Duce told me to get out and let the backhoe dig into the sand again. The foreman started digging. This time it was another five minutes before the foreman stopped. "I think we are very close to the second body. I don't want to dig further," he called out. Duce agreed, and I jumped back into the hole. This time I noticed some water slowly seeping into the area. I had the foreman drop the backhoe as close to me as possible, so I could shovel my sand into the backhoe and the foreman could put the sand into the sieve. I slowly continued to shovel the sand below my feet.

When I pushed the shovel into the wet sand about four

inches, I felt it hit something. I put the sand into the backhoe, and I carefully dug around this other object. I dug about three more shovels of sand before I switched to using my hands. I quickly found the object. Whatever it was, it was wrapped in some type of material. I had Doaks film everything as I took some close-up pictures. I had the foreman drop a tape measure to get dimensions on where the body was located. I used the seawall as a permanent marker and took the measurements from there. Once I was finished, I called out to Dr. Spock to get ready.

Spock surveyed the hole and where the body was located. He decided that he and one of his assistants would meet me when I got out of the backhoe bucket. Spock and one assistant were then lowered into the hole using the backhoe. They had their double body bag prepared for this body, but it had to be moved a little until it was freed from all the sand. Spock got the body into the bag and had the backhoe operator lower the backhoe into the hole. There were four cable hooks attached to the body bag. Once these were attached to the backhoe, the bag was slowly lifted to the surface.

Next, Spock and his assistant got into the backhoe and exited the hole. Once the bag was placed on the sand, Spock had one of his assistants head toward the medical van. Again, I checked with Doaks to see if everything had been filmed. He flipped me off but nodded his head. I was getting ready to go into the hole one more time when suddenly the entire wall on the bottom collapsed in water. Once again, I looked upward and said a silent prayer. Doaks laughed at me, "You are one lucky woman!"

"Buzz off, Doaks," I said.

Duce went over to the backhoe operator one more time. "Could you fill in the hole we just dug, then reshape the sand barrier we constructed?" he asked.

"Sure, but why are we doing this again?" the foreman asked.

"I want to be very thorough in this type of finding. I need to make sure there are no other bodies or objects down there," Duce said. Within minutes, the hole was filled, and the sand barrier was strengthened. After Duce had the foreman run the tractor over the scene one more time, he started his GPR unit. Once again, Duce slowly pushed the GPR over the area. This time, there were no objects found below the sand, and nothing appeared on his screen as he widened his grid. Then Duce expanded his grid another ten feet in one direction and five feet in another direction. Satisfied that there were no more buried objects or bodies in this area, he shut down the machine, noted the time, and told Doaks that he was finished.

Doaks said, "I'm out of here," and left the two deputies guarding the scene.

I got to my apartment around 6:00 p.m., changed clothes, and headed over to my mom and dad's condo for a late dinner.

Our conversation involved the finding of a torpedo and my finding two bodies. We were all excited, hoping to get more information on the torpedo and the bodies. It was not long before I got a phone call from Dr. Spock.

"Hood, can you come over to the office right now?" Spock requested.

"Sure, why now?" I asked.

"I think we have another homicide with the first body we dug up; the second body has not yet been X-rayed," he told me. I hung up the phone and told my mom, dad, Shane, and Allie that I had to go because the medical examiner had just discovered another possible homicide at the crime scene at the Hut. I left the condominium and headed to the medical examiner's office.

I arrived in ten minutes, exited my car, and entered the building. Doaks was not there yet, so I found Dr. Spock and started to talk. "What did you find on the first body?" I asked.

"The first victim may have been killed by that knife you found buried in the grave you discovered today. The knife was unique in its design. It was stamped with the term "KA-BAR" and measured twelve inches in length with the blade measuring seven inches long. This knife was extremely popular in World War II and had forty-two different versions. I believe this knife killed the first person we pulled out of the sand. I will await further results once I send the knife to the crime lab," Dr. Spock said.

"How did you determine that the knife killed this person?" I asked.

Spock explained, "The knife left a mark on the victim's spine directly behind the wound in his throat. I also found one other wound on the ribs around the victim's heart. These were cut, too. Whoever committed this murder knew exactly how to kill this person. I will await the findings by the DPS crime lab, but my guess is that there should be enough DNA on the knife to match our victim."

"Did you find anything else on this body?" I inquired.

"Yes, the victim had a suit on, complete with a shirt, underwear, shoes, and socks. There was no identification on him. However, I heard you found a wallet in the same grave. Have you looked at that yet?" he asked.

"No," I said. "We did find what appears to be a wallet, but I have not looked at the evidence since I put it into the evidence locker."

Dr. Spock then asked, "Do you have any theories on these two bodies?" The question threw me out of my comfort zone.

"No, not at this time," I told him. "We have a lot more investigating to do and hopefully, with some luck and some great evidence finds, we may be able to identify our first victim using the wallet," I said. "Did you photograph his clothing as well as the body?" I asked.

"Yes, the victim was male, but approximate age is unknown at this time. I need to have the crime lab do a chemical analysis of his tooth dentin to give me an age at the time of his death. He was in decent shape, and there were no other marks, scars, or tattoos on his body. I also noted on his clothing a rust-colored stain, which I believe was blood from his throat wound. There was additional staining inside his coat, which again I believe was due to the other wound on his body," Spock concluded.

"How long until you get the results back from the crime lab?" I asked.

"Hopefully within the next six to nine months," he said.

"Six to nine months!" I said, shaking my head in disgust.

"Hood, you do recall the problems we had in getting any lab results from your first homicide victim a month ago, plus look at the cost of getting the DNA results on those two babies we found!" Spock retorted.

"Of course, you are right again. I was just hoping to get some results on these two victims in less than a year!" I told him.

Spock then steered the conversation to the DNA results we sent off on the two babies we found buried below my first homicide victim at the Hut about a month ago. "What did your DNA results show regarding any possible identification of the two babies?" he asked.

"We're still waiting for the results. We had to get a search warrant requesting the records found at Ancestry.com. This business is a privately owned DNA site. The process could take about nine months to one year of waiting for their results," I told him.

Spock laughed and said, "You and I will probably have ten

or more homicides investigated by the time we get the results from your DNA search and my crime lab results!"

I shook my head and unfortunately agreed with him. I then left the medical examiner's office and headed home.

Chapter Nine:

Secret Mission

January 4, 1942, Berlin, Germany:
Almost eight decades ago

Following the bombing of Pearl Harbor on December 7, 1941, Adolf Hitler created a plan to put teams of German soldiers into the United States. Their goal was to disrupt the power grids, railroads, and bridges and to destroy arms factories. Hitler gave this plan to Admiral Wilhelm Canaris. For this assignment, the admiral was to locate and recruit nine German citizens, fluent in English, who had lived or worked or were naturalized citizens in the United States. He identified nine men.

Over the next six months, these men were trained at an intelligence school located at Quenz Lake outside of Berlin. There they were extensively trained in the use of explosives and different forms of chemical, mechanical, or electrical timing devices to set off primers in the dynamite they would be carrying as part of their mission. In their off time, each man had to memorize an extensive background history about his life in the United States. Their training lasted for months. During this time, Hitler and the admiral selected three locations along the U.S. eastern coast—Long Island, Ponte Vedra Beach, and Key Marathon—where these men would be dropped off using U-boats. The name of this mission was *Operation Pastorious.* The name "Pastorious" represented the first German settlement in the United States many decades ago. Their mission was to create internal strife in the United States. There were three missions; however, only two were known as *Operation Pastorious.* The other *secret* mission was known as *Operation Pastorious Key One.* Only four people knew about this additional mission: Hitler, Admiral Cannaris, U-202 Captain Wilhelm, and Wolf Warner (a single-person infiltrator who was part of the Kriegsmarine, with the rank of seaman).

On May 26 and 28, two submarines started their missions and headed toward these locations. Each member of these teams carried an American driver's license and other forms of identification. In addition, the men were given about $10,000 dollars in U.S. currency plus hundreds of sticks of dynamite, timing devices, and numerous weapons. There were three teams. Two teams had four men, while the Key One mission had only one man. Hitler ordered the mission to start in late June 1942. The U-boats left their ports and headed toward the United States.

U-boat 201 left Germany on May 26, 1942, and headed for Long Island. U-boat 202 left Germany on May 28, 1942, and headed toward Ponte Vedra Beach, Florida. The Long Island team arrived on the beach on June 12 late at night. The Ponte Vedra Beach team arrived on June 18, 1942. Both teams were sent ashore via rubber rafts equipped with their supplies. The last mission—the single person—swam ashore to the beach on Key Marathon, during the late evening of June 20. Because of the uniqueness of this single-person mission, a special torpedo was designed to carry all of his supplies. Once the German soldier was ashore, he signaled the U-boat captain to send the torpedo ashore. U-202 launched this specially designed torpedo about 200 yards offshore and successfully landed it on the beach. When the torpedo was ashore, the soldier unloaded all of his supplies. Once finished, the soldier floated the torpedo into the ocean, opened a valve, and sank the torpedo about twenty feet offshore. Initially all the teams had integrated into various hotels in these cities. However, the single person in Key Marathon found that there were no hotels, so he slept on the beach. Fourteen days later, the FBI received a tip and captured the first two German teams. The men were arrested and sent to a state prison. They were tried, and most were executed. The one soldier left on shore in Key Marathon was never found.

Until now.

September 19, 2021

At 7:00 a.m. on a Sunday morning, my only day off, my phone rang.

"Hood, get up!" A voice ordered. Still in a sleepy fog, my mind asked questions: *Who the heck is this? Why am I getting a call on my day off? Why did I pick up the phone?* Then I recognized the voice: Doaks!

"Doaks, why are you calling me today?" I asked.

"Get up! We have work to do on those bodies we dug up yesterday at the Hut," he ordered.

"Wait one second. Isn't this Sunday? We usually don't work on Sundays. Why are you calling me to work today?" I asked.

"The sheriff contacted me early this morning and asked what progress we had made on the two bodies we dug up yesterday. I told him we had confirmed that one was murdered and the other was still being processed. The sheriff wants a full report on the one confirmed homicide by Monday morning. So get up and meet me at the station as soon as possible." Then he hung up the phone.

I couldn't believe it. My one day off and here I was, getting up and going to work. *Crud, I just want one day off,* I thought.

I arrived at the station by 7:45 a.m. I had my to-go cup of coffee on my desk when Doaks appeared in my office.

"Hood," he said, "let's go over everything we documented at the Hut crime scene yesterday. Then let's plan our next steps in solving this case."

"Well, good morning to you too, Sgt. Doaks," I said.

"Nice to see you this early Sunday morning!" I exclaimed. Doaks shot me a glance. His eyes told me to shut up and just go with the flow, but I couldn't.

I was about to respond with an attitude, but Doaks roared, "Listen, Hood! Your job and my job is to solve homicides. The sheriff wants a report, and you and I are going to bust our hind parts to get him his report by Monday morning, so cool your attitude and let's get to work!"

Of course, Doaks was right—so I shut up, rolled my eyes, pulled out my notes from the crime scene, and we began to work. I filled Doaks in on the autopsy report I had received from Dr. Spock on our first victim. (Doaks did not make it to the autopsy briefing. I wasn't sure why, but I didn't ask and just let it slide.) I told Doaks that we did have several pieces of evidence: the knife (which I'd brought back to HQ after meeting with Spock) and the wallet, both found at the scene, and the clothing the victim was found buried in. I believed that these pieces of evidence held critical information for us in identifying our suspect and that perhaps the knife was the murder weapon. Doaks asked me where the wallet was. I told him that I thought it was in the property and evidence locker since I had put it there late Saturday afternoon.

"Well, get off your hind parts, and go get the wallet and the knife!" Doaks voice boomed at me. *One of these days*, I thought, *I am going to deck the guy, but not today*. I went to the evidence locker area, near the property and evidence rooms, and unlocked two evidence lockers with the key I had taken the night before. The evidence pieces were in the lockers. I brought both with me along with the evidence sheets.

Doaks looked at the knife, then quickly told me to put it back into evidence. The DPS lab would need to process it.

I waited a second, then asked, "I wonder if we could get any fingerprints off this knife?" He pondered that thought for a minute, then asked, "Do you think there could be a print or two on it after all this time?"

I replied, "Let's give it a try." Taking the bagged knife, we left my office and opened the crime lab door. There I took out the knife, placed it into a container, then prayed. I got my superglue going and closed the lid. Within a minute a miracle occurred: two prints appeared on the knife. One was located on the blade tip while the other was on the knife handle.

"Holy smokes!" Doaks yelled. "You were right!" Once the container was cleared, I gently took the knife out and photographed it using our digital camera. I then loaded the prints into our automatic fingerprint identification system (AFIS). Once the prints were loaded into the machine, Doaks looked at me and said, "Do you want to make a bet there are no prints that will match these in the system?"

"No," I replied. "I don't want to lose another bet to you, plus I need all of my money to keep you fed!" We left the evidence room and returned to the lab.

"OK," Doaks said. "Now let's look at this wallet." I opened a drawer in the lab and pulled out the evidence bag with the wallet inside.

"Do you think we should open it here, perhaps under some type of lamp, or use other things due to the age and the fragile state of the wallet?" I asked. Then I thought of calling Clutch—he would know. "Wait a minute," I told Doaks. "Let me call my friend Clutch."

On the first ring, Clutch picked up the phone and said, "What now, Hood?"

"Good morning, Clutch. Did I wake you?" I asked.

"No, but please tell me what you need," he said. I explained to him that we would like to open the wallet to see what kind of information (or lack of) we might find. He asked, "Was the wallet under the body?"

"No, it was on top of the body." He then asked what condition the wallet was in when I picked it out of the sieve. I told him it looked good. There were no stains, nor did I see any cuts, tears, or marks on it. Clutch told me to carefully take the wallet out of my evidence container, place it on the desk in the crime lab, open it, and let it dry. I thanked him, told him to put my request on his growing tab for dinners I owed him, and hung up.

Doaks looked at what I was doing. "Hood are you sure about this?" he asked.

"No, but Clutch seemed to think that letting the wallet air dry would be the best way to get it dried out, and then we could unfold it and see what the contents showed us," I told him.

We waited for one hour. During that time, Doaks and I

got all the clothing Dr. Spock had taken off the body. It was in an evidence locker and needed to be air dried. We took all the articles of clothing and laid them out on a large table. I was checking through the pockets on the suit jacket when I found a handkerchief. I unfolded it and placed it on the table to air dry. As I was going through another pocket, my cell phone rang. Looking at the caller ID, I saw it was my cousin Shane calling. I hit my message button, told him I was busy now, and asked him to call back later. When he called me again—this time with a 911 on his caller ID—I told Doaks to stay in the evidence room while I took the call.

"Katie, I am sorry to bother you, but I thought you should know. I was contacted by my instructor, Ret. Sgt. Major Steven Bourne. He wanted to tell me that the torpedo we found by Duck Key was a German U-boat torpedo, and it was part of a terrorist plot by Hitler to disrupt power and travel operations in the United States during World War II. I am calling you because I told him about the bodies you just found buried on the beach by the Hut. Bourne wanted me to call you ASAP to ask if there was any type of identification found on the body or in a wallet."

"Holy cow," I said. "I am at headquarters now. We are in the process of letting the wallet dry out; then I am going to open it to see what kind of identification it may contain."

Shane then asked me another strange question. "Katie, did you find a handkerchief in the clothing on the body from the crime scene?"

"Yes," I told him.

"Wow," he said, then mentioned something to Allie, his wife. Whatever he said was muffled. Then he got back on the phone to ask, "Katie, could you hold that handkerchief for a few more hours? I think my friend Bourne would like to come to your headquarters, and I think he could help you find some additional information off of that handkerchief."

"Wait," I told Shane. "Why would this guy want to come here and help me find some type of information on a handkerchief?" I asked Shane. Shane apologized, then told me some pertinent information about Bourne. He explained that Bourne was a retired Sgt. Major in the Marine Corps who had a reputation for researching most of the weaponry and secret missions of the Germans in World War II. This man was considered an expert by the U.S. Marine Corps and the Navy and was on retainer for both when needed. Shane continued, "Bourne just called me to say he had verified that the torpedo your dad and I found may have been part of another secret German mission in World War II. Bourne wanted to know if I knew anyone in the area who may be involved in investigating bodies found buried in the sand. I immediately thought of you and told Bourne that my cousin was a homicide detective at Mangrove Sheriff's Department. Bourne then asked me to contact you and see if he could meet you at the sheriff's department today, if possible, to discuss his findings. I told him I would contact you. Can he come over and talk to you?" Shane asked.

"Sure—tell him this is our headquarters address, and please tell him to come to the west door," I directed Shane.

"One more thing," Shane requested. "Once you and Bourne have met, can you please give me a call to fill me in on what you have learned?" he asked.

"Sure," I told him, then hung up. *Crud*, I thought, *Doaks will have a stroke on having yet another stranger (non-cop guy) invading our investigation.* I thought, *Tough! If this guy is an expert and can help us identify this body and help us in our investigation, then he is allowed to invade our investigation!* I left the hallway and went into the crime lab. "Doaks, we are about to have company," I told him as I closed the lab door and waited.

Chapter Ten:

Results and Mysteries

September 19, 2021

I contacted dispatch and told them I was expecting a visitor at the west door. "Please page me," I told her, "and I will meet him." Doaks was very apprehensive about letting this unknown person into our department, let alone have him involved in our homicide investigation. "Doaks, this guy is considered an expert in World War II German weaponry and secret missions. If the Marine Corps and the Navy listen to him, *you can too*, so just sit down and act decently," I told him.

Fifteen minutes later, Ret. Sgt. Major Steven Bourne met me at our west door entrance. As I introduced myself, I noted that Bourne was shorter than me, about 5'3", and had a body builders' body. He had a crew cut and a goatee and was all business. He nearly broke my hand shaking it.

"Hello, I am Retired Sergeant Major Steven Bourne, and you must be Detective Hood," he said. I returned the greeting and invited him into our office area, then into our crime lab. Doaks rose and greeted the Ret. Sgt. Major cordially.

"Hello, I am Sergeant Doaks. Glad to have you here to help us on our case," he said. I almost threw up. Doaks was being a jerk, albeit it a nice jerk, to Bourne. Bourne was all about getting to the point. He asked us the details of our finding this body and where we found the wallet and the handkerchief. Doaks was noticeably quiet during this time; then he asked Bourne, "First, can I see some type of identification to verify who you are?"

"Sure," Bourne complied, then stated, "I was expecting more than this when I got here." He continued, "If I were in your shoes, I would want to know a lot more information about me, prior to letting me walk in here and having a look at your work."

Doaks reviewed his credentials, then relaxed and looked at me. "Sorry, we were a little lax with you. So now that you've opened the conversation, I want to know what the heck makes you an expert in this area, and why should we listen to anything you tell us?" Doaks ordered.

Bourne thanked Doaks for the clarification and gave us a short background of his military service and his work as a computer analyst in intelligence. He then proceeded to tell us more about the torpedo Shane and my dad had found. He showed us a copy of Hitler's secret order involving nine German marines landing in the United States to disrupt our power grids and our transportation systems. Doaks asked him where he found all of this information. Bourne said that he worked as a computer intelligence specialist for all branches of our armed services. He had access to a number of databases and files that revealed a possible explanation for this secret mission.

Doaks then asked, "Did you get any of this information off the onion router (TOR)?"

Bourne stared at him for a minute, then said, "I have my sources, but if I tell you, I would have to kill you—so I cannot reveal where I got this information." There were a few long seconds of silence. "Just kidding," Bourne said, then laughed. "You set yourself up for that one. I have always wanted to do that, so thanks for letting me scare you for a nanosecond!"

Crud, I thought, *this guy is a lot of fun but kind of spooky.*

Doaks looked at him again, then grinned. "You're right—I was expecting something like that from you," then laughed along with Bourne.

"OK, now that all the fun and games are over, can we get down to solving this case?" I asked. Doaks, then Bourne, nodded in agreement, and we began. The first thing Bourne asked was to see the handkerchief.

"Why the handkerchief?" Doaks asked.

"Well, according to my research, if this body was part of this secret mission, then the handkerchief has invisible ink that tells the details of this mission."

"Wait a second," I said. "Invisible ink?"

"Yes, Hitler was a fanatic about hiding details and loved to use invisible ink on handkerchiefs to remind his subordinates what their missions were," Bourne said.

"So, do you think that after all these years in the sand and water there might be some details about this mission left on the handkerchief?" I asked.

"I don't know, but if you have some chemicals or an ultraviolet light in this lab, I believe it is worth checking," Bourne said.

Doaks said, "Do you think we could use an ultraviolet light first, prior to getting out the chemicals?"

"It's worth a try," Bourne said. I was in shock. How did Doaks know this stuff? Where did he read or find out about invisible ink?

"OK, let's see what happens," Doaks said as he placed the dried handkerchief on the large table. As the room became darker, and under the ultraviolet light, some type of writing appeared on the handkerchief. Bourne and Doaks looked at the writing; both concluded it was German. Bourne then asked Doaks if he knew or could read and translate German. Doaks said, "No, but let's take a picture. Then we can locate someone who can translate this message." Bourne waited until several pictures were taken. I was shocked to see a message, in German, still visible on this handkerchief after all these years.

Bourne asked Doaks' permission to make a call. Doaks asked, "Who are you calling?"

"I have a contact, an expert German translator who uses TOR. These people are a husband-and-wife team, Ricky and

Lucy, who could translate this message in seconds." Doaks nodded his head in approval, and Bourne placed the call. Within seconds, Bourne sent a text with the pictures attached to Ricky and Lucy. And in minutes, they answered with this response:

Translated from German to English:

> *You are to proceed with the operational plan discussed during your training: blow up bridges connecting the Keys to the mainland, destroy any power lines or water supply lines, and kill anyone who tries to stop you. You must return to your pickup location in 30 days, or you will be left on shore.*

Bourne then told Doaks to please take a picture of their response because it would disappear in one minute—as would their phone number and any record of their contact to his phone. *Crap*, I thought. Bourne must have sensed some frustration on my face.

"Hood, you looked puzzled," he said.

"Yes," I replied. "Disappearing texts and phone contacts, no history—this is like a *Mission Impossible* movie!"

"Yes," he said, "a reality today and something most people do not know exists." Bourne asked Doaks if we had opened the wallet.

"No, not yet," Doaks said, "but let's open it now and see what we can find—if anything." Doaks then asked me to put on new gloves and slowly open the wallet. The wallet appeared to be dried out with no tears and no marks. I slowly opened it.

"Whoa," I exclaimed. "There are some pictures here and a driver's license and some type of other identification." Doaks and Bourne looked over my shoulder, and both remarked how well preserved these items were. I then opened several more areas in the wallet. On the back fold, I found an identification card with a picture of a man identified as Wolf Werner.

Bourne jumped in: "I have researched this mission, and I believe you will find this man's body is Wolf Werner. He was a member of the German Navy, a Kriegsmarine, with the rank of seaman. He was twenty-one at the time of this mission. His physical characteristics were height: six feet, weight: one-ninety, eyes: hazel, hair: brown. His home address was Hamburg, Germany." Bourne then showed us a picture of this man and a detailed report on his background.

Doaks looked at Bourne and asked, "Where did you find this information?" Bourne smiled and told us that he had done some research on secret missions involving Germany in World War II. During his research, he found some information on Operation Pastorious. This mission had two parts: one was to drop off two teams of four men each onto the shorelines of Long Island, New York, and Ponte Vedra Beach in Florida. After digging deeper, he'd found a second mission that involved dropping off one man in Key Marathon. This man was an expert in explosives and was known as the "Wolf."

Bourne continued, "I contacted some friends, who, after digging in a number of known and unknown databases on the Web and TOR, found this information on Wolf Werner."

"So, what led you to research this person?" I asked.

"The torpedo your cousin and your dad found off Duck Key," he said. "Once I was contacted by the Navy regarding this torpedo find, I went to the Coast Guard Cutter holding the torpedo, examined the weapon, and concluded that it was a 1942 version of a German WW II model. The torpedo was modified with no explosives. Instead there was space so that the payload for this mission could be packed inside, then launched onto the shoreline. Once I discovered this was a German WWII torpedo modified for a special mission, I began my research." It was from this torpedo that Bourne learned about this secret mission and who was involved.

"Wow!" Doaks exclaimed. "You are telling us that this man may be part of a secret World War II mission that Hitler planned and executed in 1942?"

"Yes, exactly—and unfortunately no one knows about this mission, and there may be more information you find as you continue your investigation." Bourne said.

Doaks sat down and rubbed his head, "Hood, what else did you find in this wallet?"

I again was slowly turning over each of the small plastic pocket containers when I saw something sticking out behind one of the photographs. I got a pair of tweezers and slowly pulled out a piece of paper. On the paper was a map of some kind. "Hey, can both of you come over here and look at this?" I asked. Bourne and Doaks came over and looked at the piece of paper. On the paper was a crude drawing showing a bridge and an X. There was nothing else on the paper.

Doaks said, "What the h- -l is this?" I shook my head, but Bourne looked again at the piece of paper. He asked, "Can you take me to the crime scene location of the body?"

"Sure, we can take you now, if you want," Doaks said. I locked the crime lab door, and we all left the area. We arrived at the Hut in fifteen minutes. Doaks was out of the car and walking toward our crime scene before Bourne and I had stepped out.

We arrived at the scene, and Bourne asked us one more question: "In 1942, what was built in this location?"

"Nothing," Doaks responded. "Nothing was built on this beach until the late 1950s."

"What buildings existed along the roadway in 1942?" Bourne asked.

Doaks scratched his head again and stated, "I believe there were only a few buildings along the road. There was an old restaurant/store called 'Ye Ole Fleshing Hole.' That was about it, except for some shacks, temporary buildings where people could sleep and live temporarily."

Bourne then asked us, "So there was only one bridge in this area then?"

"Yes, there was only one bridge then, and there is only one bridge now, called the 'Vaca Cut Bridge,'" Doaks explained.

Bourne asked, "If there was only one bridge in the area, then I believe the map on the piece of paper Hood found is a map of Vaca Cut Bridge—and I believe we may be able to find what the X means on that map."

"Wait one second here," Doaks stated. "You think that paper with a map Hood just pulled out of the wallet is the Vaca Cut Bridge?"

"Yes," said Bourne. "Can we go there now?"

"Sure," Doaks replied, "but I don't have a picture of the map now."

"I got you covered, Doaks," I said. "Let's go."

On the way over to the Vaca Cut Bridge, Bourne told us what we might find buried near the bridge. "My research indicates that we should find some dynamite, some timing devices, some money, and some weapons."

"Crap," Doaks said. "Old dynamite is very unstable. It could blow up if we aren't careful digging."

Bourne smiled again, then said, "I have contacted our Navy demolition team to meet us at the bridge location in fifteen minutes."

"What?" I said. "Your Navy demolition team is coming to the bridge in fifteen minutes?" I repeated.

"I believe it is in our national interest to locate this site and remove any dangerous explosives or other items that may jeopardize the safety of the citizens in the area and the stability of the bridge."

"S- -t," Doaks said, "I must contact the sheriff on this. He will not like having the Navy or any other demolition team digging up explosives in his jurisdiction."

Bourne smiled again. "I contacted the admiral in charge

of this area, and he contacted your sheriff about three minutes ago. The sheriff will be meeting us at the bridge location in about a minute."

Doaks looked at me and then back at Bourne sitting in the backseat. "Who are you?"

Bourne just smiled again and said, "I am just an old Retired Sergeant Major in the Marine Corps."

Two minutes later we arrived at the bridge, where we were surprised to find several deputies, the sheriff, the bomb squad commander, and the SWAT commander waiting. Some of these deputies had begun to cone off part of the bridge. "Good afternoon, Doaks, Hood, and you must be Ret. Sgt. Major Bourne," the sheriff said, shaking all of our hands. "Please tell me, Ret. Sgt. Major Bourne, what are we going to find here?"

For the next fifteen minutes, Bourne debriefed the sheriff and the command staff on what he expected we would find at the scene. Doaks again looked at me and asked, "Who is this guy?"

I shook my head. "I don't know, but whoever he is, we need to listen to him!"

The Navy demolition team arrived in two black Chevy Suburbans. Everyone exchanged greetings; then a lieutenant took charge of his men and directed them down to the sand under the bridge. Within minutes, the demolition team produced several ground penetrating radar machines and several metal detectors. Immediately all of these men were working in an area north of the bridge. "I got something here," one of the demo team members shouted. The lieutenant and several team members looked at the ground penetrating radar screen and saw a large box. Bourne then told the Navy men to get their tools and be careful digging into this site.

Meanwhile, Bourne suggested that we all move away from the dig site and go into our air-conditioned cars. Bourne stated that he would let us all know what was found once the area was secured. Doaks and I joined the sheriff and his two commanders in his Ford Expedition.

"Who is this guy Bourne?" one of the commanders asked.

He responded, "I don't know, but I can tell you that I have never been called by the admiral in charge of this area—and the governor—about this case, so whoever Bourne is, we will all listen to him, got it?" All heads in the car nodded, and again Doaks looked at me, whispering, "Who is this guy?"

Fifteen minutes had passed when a text appeared on the sheriff's phone: "All clear. Please come down to the scene." Immediately, all of us left the sheriff's car and walked down toward Bourne. Once we all arrived, Bourne explained what was found and the implications of the find to our country. Bourne stated that the box the Navy men found contained about 1,000 pounds of dynamite, six timing devices, and three weapons. There was also about $8,000 cash in American one-hundred-dollar bills. The dynamite was very unstable but was rendered safe by the demo team, while all of the timing devices, weapons, and money were secured by the Navy team.

Bourne then asked the sheriff for a word in private. The

sheriff and Bourne left the area for about five minutes. When the sheriff returned, he ordered Doaks and me to take pictures of everything, then prepare a follow-up report on the findings. The sheriff stated that this property belonged to the U.S. Navy and would not be used as evidence in this case until he was notified by the governor. Doaks and I took pictures of everything, then turned to thank Bourne.

Bourne was not there. He had left. All of the deputies had cleared the bridge and then left the area. Doaks and I returned to his car and again looked at each other, wondering who is this guy, and what had just happened? We went back to headquarters, completed our follow-up reports as directed by the sheriff, and went home.

Later that evening, I contacted my cousin Shane and filled him in on what happened after his phone call that morning.

"Very interesting," Shane said. "I might have some more information on this later this month. I have to make a few more phone calls, and thanks for getting back to me. Enjoy your evening," and he hung up.

I poured a glass of wine and again asked myself, *Who is this guy Bourne?*

Chapter Eleven:
Fusion Centers and Results

September 20, 2021

I arrived at the office at 7:45 a.m. Doaks was not there yet, but O'Neill came into my office and sat down.

"Hood, I need to pick your brain on a few things. Is this a good time?" he inquired.

"Sure, how can I assist you?" I responded. For the next thirty minutes, his few things covered a lot of areas. He wanted to know who the Bourne guy was. I explained to him about my initial contact with Bourne as well as what occurred on Sunday; how the sheriff had reacted to Bourne's requests regarding the hidden box of dynamite, weapons, and money; and how the Navy responded. Next, he wanted to pick my brain about the use of a fusion center to assist our task force in finding Maria. I told him I had limited knowledge of fusion centers but thought that Clutch would be an excellent resource in getting a fusion center involved in helping us.

Then he wanted to know my theories on where I thought Maria Hernandez was living.

I scratched my head, took a long pause, and leveled with him. "I believe that Maria is living in a country that has a non-extradition treaty with our country. Maria has lived in the Keys most, if not all, of her life, which leads me to believe that she is living in a country that has an environment similar to the Keys. I also believe we need to go over the evidence left in Commander Lopez's vehicle. I recall that the forensic nurse, Laszacko, found something tucked into the front seat belt buckle, but I can't remember what it was now—too many other things happened this weekend," I told him.

O'Neill nodded his head in agreement with everything I said. Then he asked me another question. "Would you like to go out for a drink with me later this week?"

Holy crap, I thought to myself, *am I missing something here? I will not date anyone in the police business, and what's going on with O'Neill?* "Ah, I need to get back to you on that," I hesitated in my answer.

"Great," O'Neill said and left my office.

Clutch called a meeting of the task force at 10:00 a.m. At this meeting Clutch wanted to go over some updated information our task force had discovered, and he wanted to update us on a fusion center becoming part of our investigation. Doaks looked at me with a big question on his mind: *What the h - -l is a fusion center?* I was about to whisper my answer when a new person was introduced to the task force.

"This is Assistant Director of Criminal Intelligence for our DPS agency. Please welcome Mr. Eric Johnson," Clutch stated. Johnson greeted each of us with a firm handshake, then began to inform us on what a fusion center is and how it works. Forty minutes later, Johnson asked if anyone had any questions. No one responded, and he asked Clutch if it was ok to take a quick break. Clutch told everyone to take five minutes and then come back to our conference room.

Doaks was jabbing me in the ribs. "Hood, did you understand any of this junk?"

I told Doaks, "Let's step outside the conference room and get a cup of coffee." We were pouring two cups of coffee when Eric Johnson came by and asked us if we could talk. We nodded. Then Mr. Johnson—Eric, as he asked us to call him—began to pick my brain on where I thought Maria Hernandez was living. Before I could answer, Doaks asked Eric to please give him a short version on what a fusion center does and how it could possibly help our investigation. Eric did a great job explaining fusion centers, how they work in helping law enforcement find wanted individuals, and how they have prevented numerous terrorist attacks in our country since 2001. Doaks was impressed and thanked Eric sincerely.

I was in shock. Doaks had just met this guy, who was not a cop, yet here Doaks was accepting him as a brother in policing. I questioned myself: *Is Doaks going through a change of life now?* Eric then picked my brain on where I thought Maria was hiding and why. He told us thanks and left the break room.

When our five-minute break was over, Doaks and I headed back to the conference room. Clutch then told us that Eric would give us some updated information about Maria. Eric proceeded to tell us that the fusion center—working with Interpol, the FBI, CIA, NSA, the National Police in Spain, and a few other global government intelligence agencies—had generated some new information on the possible location of Maria Hernandez. Eric showed us a number of possible locations where the climate and the environment in these countries were similar to the Florida Keys. In addition, he added another factor: that these countries had a non-extradition treaty with the United States.

He then shared two other pieces of information he had just learned. First, the body of Selena's husband had just been identified in Cambodia. Interpol, working with two other unnamed global agencies, had identified the body of Mr. Rodriquez, Selena's husband. According to these sources, he was tortured and then murdered. His body was found in the city of Sihanoukville, Cambodia. It was apparently dumped into a trash container adjacent to a restaurant called Khin's Shack. The report also stated that his body was mutilated and that the local police had a difficult time identifying him. Eric stated that this type of death indicated that the drug cartels in the area may be involved because they were known by their various methods of killing their victims. Next, he said the body of ex-commander Juan Lopez was recently found in Saigon, Vietnam. His body was placed inside a grease container for the Vo Roof Garden Restaurant in Saigon. The police investigation indicated that there were numerous signs of trauma on his body; however, the autopsy performed by the medical examiner in Saigon appeared to indicate that he was poisoned, then tortured, then mutilated.

Ex-commander Lopez was poisoned. I pondered whether it was possible that Maria was involved in this murder too. My mind drifted from the briefing, and I thought about the types of poisons available in Vietnam. I was just going to make a note when Eric called on me.

"Det. Hood, would you like to add any information to our theory on where Maria may be hiding out?"

"No," I stammered, trying to regain my cool. Clutch thanked Eric, who then sat down.

Clutch continued, "We may have one more lead on finding Maria's possible location. Nurse Laszacko found a cigar wrapper stuck in the front driver's side seat belt. The wrapper was from a cigar shop in Vietnam. Now we find the body of ex-commander Lopez in a restaurant in Saigon, Vietnam? There are too many coincidences here. I want Hood, Doaks, and O'Neill working on trying to find some type of connection to Maria's possible location in Vietnam. I want Burns, Laszacko, and Hudson reviewing all of the evidence collected from Lopez's vehicle, and I want Lincoln and Colonel Ortez coordinating their efforts on getting more information on the deaths of Rodriquez and Lopez. In addition, I want Hood and

O'Neill speculating on possible locations in Vietnam where Maria Hernandez may be living now." The meeting ended with Clutch setting a due date of two days to complete our work assignments and meet again on September 22 at 9:00 a.m.

Doaks, O'Neill, and I left the conference area and headed toward my office. Doaks excused himself and went to the men's room while O'Neill and I continued on. In my office, O'Neill looked at me and asked, "What about the poison found in Lopez's body?"

"Dang," I said, "am I that obvious?"

"Yes, I saw your reaction to Eric's question, and you were clearly zoned out once the cause of death involved poison," O'Neill said.

I then began to think out loud. I rattled off several ideas to O'Neill and then Doaks when he returned. "What kind of poisonous plants grow in Vietnam? How could a simple poison be made from one of these plants? Do any poisonous plants grow near Saigon? How can we verify the work of the medical examiner in Saigon? Does the restaurant where Lopez was found have any video recording equipment? How can we get a copy of it? How could we find where Lopez was living, and have any other pieces of evidence been left by Lopez if he was living in Saigon?"

O'Neill shook his head. "Great questions, Hood." Then he turned to Doaks. "Anything to add?"

Doaks looked away for a second and then asked O'Neill, "Can you get someone in your agency to try to hack into the video in that restaurant in Saigon to see if we can find Lopez and the person he was eating with?"

O'Neill thought about his request. "I believe I can find someone to do what you want, but I need some time," he stated. He then got up and left my office.

"Nice question, Doaks," I said, slapping him on the back. "I just might get you thinking about forensics yet!" Doaks didn't respond but told me to get to work. Then he left my office.

It was now 12:00 p.m., and I was starving. I was heading out the door when Doaks stopped me and asked, "Going somewhere? Come on, let's go to Rosa's. I'm starving, and today is their taco plate special."

While we were eating at Rosa's, Doaks began to ask me several questions. "Hood, where do you think Maria is living now? Are you going to look into the poisons, or do you want me to do that? What do you think I can do to help on this investigation, and I will pick up the tab on this lunch!"

"Wait, one second," I said, "you are going to pick up the *tab*?" I began to seriously wonder about Doaks, picking up the tab for the first time in all the years we had been working together.

"That's right," Doaks boasted, "and I am giving you a promotion to Detective—no more Rookie status!" My mouth must have dropped to the table and onto the dirty floor. *Holy crap*, I thought, *Doaks is having a mental breakdown. I need to reaffirm what I just was told!*

"So, Doaks, let me understand what just occurred. First you want to pick up the tab, and now I am no longer going to be referred to as 'Rookie,'" I said, astonished.

"Shut up, Hood, I was only teasing you. Here, you can pick up the tab, Rookie!" Doaks was laughing out loud now. *Crud! Well, now I know Doaks isn't cracking up just yet.* I took care of the bill, and we left.

Back at headquarters, I began researching poisonous plants growing in the Saigon area. After a quick Google search, I found that there is one plant known as *heartbreak grass* or *la ngon*, which is the most poisonous plant in Vietnam. Three leaves of this plant in a soup or drink can kill a man in one hour or less. That caught my immediate attention. Next, I contacted O'Neill to ask, "Can we get a copy of the autopsy report, and was a toxicology report done on Lopez?"

O'Neill came over to my office, sat down, and closed my door. *What the heck is this*, I asked myself. "Hood, I need to confess something to you," he said. "I have found out that the autopsy report on Lopez is being held by the Saigon Police Department, and I don't know a way to get the report released to us."

"So, we are back to square one on our investigation into Lopez's death as well as any additional information," I replied.

"Yes, my contacts in the Bureau have not been able to find a way to hack into the Saigon Police Records Unit to get a copy of the report and the autopsy," he stated grudgingly.

"Interesting," I said. "Then how did Eric get his information?"

"Great question," O'Neill answered. "He got access somehow to the police report but not the autopsy or tox screen report."

"Did you tell Clutch about this dilemma?" I asked.

"No, why?" he asked. I then explained how Clutch works and how he could find the right people to get information when he needed it to solve a case.

O'Neill was just about to get up when Doaks came running down the hall to my office, threw open my door, and said, "We all need to get into the conference room now. Clutch has an important announcement for all of us." We all left my office and met in the conference room.

Once we were all seated, Clutch stood and announced, "We have just received some information relating to the deaths of Mr. Rodriquez and Juan Lopez. According to our fusion center director, Eric, both deaths appear to be tied to a large drug cartel run by Mr. Z. Mr. Z., as he is called, was recently arrested, but he escaped from the jail in Saigon last week. He has disappeared into the jungles of Vietnam." According to Eric, an informant with the Vietnam police and Interpol had told his superiors that both men (Lopez and Rodriquez) were trying to start their own drug business in the Saigon area. Both tried to undercut Mr. Z's organization, and both were killed in different ways. The informant also stated that there was a woman involved in the killing of Lopez. The woman appeared to be an American, Hispanic female, very attractive, who had experience in poisoning people. Eric then stated that his organization was coordinating with an undisclosed agency within the U.S. Intelligence Community (IC). They had received a copy of the video in which Lopez was sharing a meal with this woman. The video had been obtained from an unknown government intelligence agency that hacked into the restaurant in the Saigon video system. Eric continued, "Unfortunately, we do not have a good enough picture of this woman's face to use our facial recognition system to identify her."

Doaks raised his hand. "Are there more videos at this restaurant, perhaps at their entrance, or in a hallway, or in a garage adjacent to the restaurant?"

Eric paused before answering, checked his notes on his phone, and then responded, "There were no other video cameras in those locations. We identified a bank located across the entrance to the restaurant. Unfortunately, the bank did not have any video equipment at that location."

I nodded my head to Doaks and whispered, "Good thought!"

Eric then sat down, and Clutch took over the meeting. "OK, let's keep looking into those areas I assigned you. Please keep digging—I expect some answers by 9/22."

Chapter Twelve:

Kris Connection

September 20, 2021

Approximately 9,950 miles away from Key Marathon, Selena Rodriquez (aka Maria Hernandez) had started to established her new life in Vung Tau, Vietnam. She was working her way up in a drug organization run by a Mr. Z and had begun her own criminal connections in Saigon. She was living in a small villa near a resort in Vung Tau. Her life was adjusting and somewhat like her prior life in the Keys. Her fame as a ruthless crime boss and a player in the drug distribution industry was growing. She needed about one more year until she would regain all of her losses from the disaster at the Hut. However, her world was about to change as a new family from America moved into a resort apartment adjacent to her villa.

The Bird family had just arrived at the Marina Bay Resort and Spa in Vung Tau, Vietnam. Paul Bird was the new manager for this resort and had decided to bring his family along for this new employment venture. Paul had been married to Kris for the past twenty-seven years. The Bird family had six children—four natural kids, two adopted twin boys—and one big mutt, Fang. Fang was a mongrel mix of Rottweiler, Irish Wolfhound, and Boxer. He was called Fang because of his underbite: it showed his big canine teeth on each side of his lips. Fang had been with the family for the past five years. Going to Vietnam, then being quarantined for 30 days, was typical in the life of Fang and the Bird family. Paul had taken this job as a pre-retirement job for the next twelve months to help his motel's parent company get reestablished in this area. Four of the Birds' children had "left their nest" and were living on their own. One was married, two were in college, and one was going to veterinary school. The twin boys Mark and Matty, had been working with their dad in getting their sailing certifications on multiple sailing ships.

Kris and Paul had been anticipating this pre-retirement move for the past five years. The opening at this resort provided Paul with a great way to cap off his retirement package and to complete his American Sailing Association (ASA) Level 106 certification on advanced coastal cruising. Paul had done a lot of planning prior to taking this job. His company had agreed to give him a severance/retirement package following his twenty-five years of service. He also anticipated completing his last sailing test and purchasing a large catamaran. His goal was to sail back to the United States sometime after June 2023 when he was scheduled to retire. After years of living in the Denver,

Colorado area, Kris and the boys—Mark and Matty—were still adjusting to this new type of climate. Vietnam was not cold, always comfortable, with lots of sunshine and humidity. The humidity was an issue for everyone in the Bird family. Over the next few weeks, Kris and her boys spent a lot of time adjusting to their new home and swimming in the bay.

One day Kris was outside having coffee when she heard someone singing. Kris remembered this song from her high school days in Quito, Ecuador. The song was a Spanish love song. Kris listened until the woman had finished the song, then hollered over to her, "Buenos Dias, mi amiga." The woman then turned in Kris's direction and spoke back the same greeting.

For the next fifteen minutes, the woman and Kris conversed in Spanish. Their conversation was about the weather, the children in their lives, and what brought them both to this resort. Then Matty began calling for Kris, so she left, apologizing in Spanish, to see what Matty needed.

Over the next few days, Kris and the woman (Kris didn't know her name) had daily conversations in Spanish. These conversations consisted of some common questions about where they were born, where they grew up, where their families were living, and how they both ended up living in Vietnam. Kris enjoyed talking to another woman, particularly in Spanish, because she was still in the process of learning Vietnamese.

One day Kris headed over to see if her new friend was hanging her laundry outside. When she got close to the wall separating both houses, she saw three men walking into the woman's kitchen area. There she saw that each man had a machine gun strapped under his suitcoat jackets. In addition, she saw one man handing over to her a large gym bag of something. Upon closer examination she saw that the bag contained lots of American money. As she continued to watch, one of the men told her friend in a very loud voice, "The Tongs are coming for you! Your daughter is now in the ocean in pieces, and you are next!" The men left the kitchen, then exited the area.

Hearing this and seeing the actions of these men, Kris immediately left the area and went back to her apartment. There she called her husband, Paul, to relate what had happened. Since both boys were out sailing in the bay, Kris wondered what she should do with this information. She immediately thought of calling her dad. Her dad was a retired cop, supervisor, commander, and police chief with over 30 years of experience in various states and the U.S. Army Military Police Corps. If she were still living in Denver, she would have immediately called him. But now she was living in Vietnam and her dad was living in Texas. Dad was about eight hours behind her current time. She decided to wait until later in the day to call him. Kris thought more about what she observed, then said to herself, "Dad would tell me to report all of these actions to the local police." However, in Vietnam, Kris did not know any of the local authorities, nor could she speak any Vietnamese. Following a short conversation with Paul, he too suggested that she call her dad later in the day to ask his advice.

In Key Marathon, Florida, it was 1:30 in the morning. Forensic Nurse Colleen Laszacko was still going over the pieces of evidence she had found in Lopez's vehicle. She was also thinking about the updated reports on the deaths of Lopez and Rodriquez. Both men were killed in the Golden Triangle drug area—one in Thailand and the other in Saigon, Vietnam. Both men were tortured, one was poisoned, and both were involved with Maria Hernandez. Laszacko was still thinking about these things when she decided to call her sister who had just moved to Vung Tau, Vietnam. Kris answered the call on the second ring.

"Hey, Sista, how are things in Vietnam?" Colleen asked.

"Uh, we are doing ok. A little different moving here compared to the last move from Phoenix to Denver. We are still adjusting to the weather, and the humidity is a killer—especially for my hair," Kris laughed. "So, how is your case going? Any luck finding the chick who killed a lot of people and those police officers?"

"Funny you should ask," Colleen said. "I have been up most of the night trying to figure out if this Maria chick is somewhere in Vietnam," she stated.

"Why Vietnam?" Kris asked.

Colleen sighed and begrudgingly rehashed the most recent ponderings of what she had been dealing with, evidence she had found in the suspect's car, updated information on the deaths of two men, both directly involved with Maria. Kris's interest piqued, and she wanted to know more about this woman. What did she look like? How old was she? What kind of mannerisms or unique personal traits did this woman have? Colleen answered her questions and painted a vivid picture for Kris's mind to see. After hearing all of this, Kris excitedly described her next-door neighbor. In rapid-fire sentences, she told Colleen about her most recent interactions with her neighbor and the three men who had just visited her.

While Kris was talking, Colleen quickly scrolled through her phone images and asked if she could send her a picture of Maria Hernandez.

Kris said, "Uh yeah, duh." They filled the time waiting with a quick update on the kids and families. Colleen paused the conversation when she heard the ding telling her that Kris had received the photo. "Holy frijoles!" Kris shouted. "That is the woman living next door to me *now*!"

Colleen shouted, "Holy crap, Kris, are you sure it's her?"

"Yes, it is definitely her. I can't believe it! What should I do now?"

"Hold tight, stay on the line, and don't freak out. I am calling my boss. I want him on a conference call with you now!" Colleen put Kris on hold. Three minutes later a guy named Clutch and another guy named O'Neill were on the conference call with Kris and Colleen. Both men introduced themselves to Kris before barraging her with some very specific questions about the woman she had been talking to over the past few days. After all their questions were answered,

Kris enthusiastically shared the actions and the words she had heard that day while observing the men talking to the woman next door.

"Crap," Clutch barked into the phone, "if the Tong organization was mentioned during the conversation along with the revelation that they killed Maria's daughter, Salsa, and now they are coming after Maria, we need to get a plan of action together to detain Maria ASAP."

Clutch and O'Neill thanked Kris for her actions, told her to call them if she observed any other activity, and hung up. Colleen stayed on the phone, shaking her head in disbelief. "Holy crap. I still cannot wrap my head around this. My sister is living next door to a wanted felon, and now she is involved in the same case I am! Of course this would happen to her—never a dull moment in the Bird household," Colleen quipped.

As the initial shock began to wear off and some potential fear started to sink in, it was Kris's turn to shake her head. Her new acquaintance was a very dangerous, wanted woman. After a deep breath, Kris said, "All right, Sister, what the heck do I do now? Should I be concerned for our safety and high tail it back to Colorado?"

Colleen chuckled. "Slow down, Sista. Just try to be your friendly neighborly self." Anxious to get moving but not wanting to shrug her sister off, Colleen continued, "We have a lot to process now, but I will do my best to keep you posted. But in the meantime, you do zip—nothing. When Paul gets home, go somewhere privately and fill him in, but *please* don't tell the boys anything. This woman may look nice, but listen: she is ruthless. One other thing—does the resort have a security camera system?" Colleen asked.

Kris thought for a second, then said, "Let me call Paul and see. I am sure we have some type of security cameras. I will check and call you back."

Colleen told her, "If possible, just keep an eye on her villa, and please promise to call me if you see or suspect anything suspicious—like her leaving with a gym bag or a suitcase." Then, pointedly, Colleen asked, "Kris, you cool with that?"

" Yes, yes, we'll be fine, and I'll be on the lookout. Go solve your case and rid the world of bad guys and girls. Love you, Sis. Talk soon." Kris gently hit the "End" button and thought, *Well, isn't this just great. How in the heck is Paul going to react to this?* With a new set of eyes and a different purpose, Kris peered out her window looking over at the small villa.

Paul called Kris five minutes after she and Colleen had finished talking. Kris filled him in on the woman living next door and then asked him about hotel security cameras. Paul called an office and asked for a Mr. Dung. Mr. Dung was head of security for the resort. Paul told Kris he would call her back in a few, then hung up. In the next five minutes, Mr. Dung located the tapes from the past several days. He and Paul then looked at three specific days and times to see if the outside perimeter camera caught any pictures of Kris talking with this woman—Selena. After some time, there in the camera was a clear picture of Kris talking to this woman. Paul and

Mr. Dung continued looking and found two additional video recordings showing Kris talking to the woman.

Paul called Kris and gave her the news. "What should we do with these tapes?" he asked.

"Let me call Colleen and see how she wants to process this new information." Paul agreed and hung up. Kris called Colleen again and told her about the video tapes. Colleen told her to hang on while she contacted a Mr. Johnson at the Fusion Center.

Eric Johnson answered on the third ring. Colleen created another conference call between Eric, Colleen, and Kris. Eric introduced himself to Kris and took down some information. Then he asked Kris for a direct line to Paul and Mr. Dung. Eric told the sisters that he was going to arrange for these video tapes to be copied remotely. Then he hung up.

"Listen, Colleen, what's next? What should I do in the next few hours? Any suggestions would be most helpful now that I have the poop scared out of me!"

"Kris, just try to be yourself. I know that may be hard to do now, but just be you," Colleen instructed. "I will keep you posted on what these guys will be doing when I can. In the meantime, you do your thing there. Again, if you see something like this woman leaving, please note as much information as you can, then call me!"

"What type of information are you asking me to look for?" Kris asked.

"Look at what this woman is carrying with her—a suitcase,

some small bags, etc. Then note what kind of transportation she left in—cab, car, etc. See if anyone is with her. If so, get a complete description—you know, like dad taught us!"

"OK, then what?"

"Note what time of day she left and what day of the week," Colleen said.

"Great, I will do all of this. Anything else?" Kris asked.

"Sista, be cool. You can do this job without freaking out—look at what you all have been through. This is typical stuff for you and your crazy family to be involved in." Kris sighed as she thought about this. Colleen was right: their family had gone through a lot of crazy things in the past twenty-seven years. This was just one more memory to add to their family's legacy.

"OK, Sista, I am ready to help you solve this case and catch this woman. Talk to you soon. Love ya." Kris hung up. *Great*, Kris thought to herself, *here we are living by a wanted ruthless person, who has now wrecked my day here in Vietnam. What's next?*

Chapter Thirteen:

Maria's Escape and Pieces Falling into Place

September 27, 2021—10:00 p.m.

Kris had been very busy—first preparing dinner for her family, then watching the villa next door, then putting Mark and Matty to bed. All of this ended around 9:55 p.m. Kris decided she and Paul would have a glass of wine on the back porch. As she was pouring wine, she thought she heard a noise coming from the villa. She ran upstairs into their bedroom in time to see a person leaving the villa. Kris was not sure if this person was a man or woman. She did notice that the person was walking with a limp and carrying a cane. She also saw that the person was putting two small carry-on bags and one gym bag into the trunk of a taxi. Once the person was in the cab, the person mumbled a few words to the driver, who then shut the trunk and left. Putting the wine glasses aside on her desk, she called Colleen. Colleen picked up the phone on the third ring.

"Hello," she groggily said.

"Sista, rise and shine, there is movement at the villa! Someone just left, and I need to know what to do next!" Kris was yelling into the phone.

"Dude, it is the middle of the night here, and my systems are not firing on all cylinders yet. Give me a second and quit yelling at me." Rubbing her eyes and attempting to sit up, Colleen said, "Excuse me for trying to sleep, and, good Lord, what time is it anyway?"

Animated and very loudly, Kris said, "Who cares about the time? Maria has left, or I think it was her. Anyway, someone just left the villa using a cab. The person squished two small flight bags and one gym bag into the taxi's trunk. The person was walking with a limp and using a cane."

"Kris, take a deep breath, slow down, and allow me to clear the cobwebs from my slumber. Maybe bring it down an octave or two, ok?" Colleen asked. "OK, so let me get this straight. A person just left the villa and shoved some bags in a trunk, correct? So what happened next?" Colleen asked.

"Well, this person got into the cab and took off," Kris stated.

"OK, can you see the villa from where you are standing right now?" Colleen asked.

"Yes."

"OK, do you see anything on? Lights, television flickering, anything to indicate someone may still be there?" Colleen asked.

"Nothing that I can see. It appears that no one is there," Kris told her.

"Kris, do you remember if either the driver or the person said anything to each other? Did it look like they were having a conversation or just small talk?"

"Let me think. Umm, wait—I did hear something like 'con them.' The person yelled that to the driver," Kris recalled.

"Con them," Colleen repeated.

"Yes, that is what I heard, or something very close to that," Kris said.

"OK, what were you doing before you called me?" Colleen asked.

"Pouring Paul and me a glass of red wine. We were about to sit on our back porch," Kris said.

"OK, go enjoy your glass of wine on the porch. Sit tight and let me figure out what to do next. I will call you back after I call my boss and see what he wants you to do next." Colleen thanked Kris and hung up.

Colleen sauntered to the bathroom, turned on some lights, and splashed some very cold water onto her face. Looking in the mirror, she said, "Please, Lord, give me the strength and energy to start my day at this godforsaken hour!" Shaking the sleepiness away, her brain jumped into overdrive, and she dialed Clutch's cell phone.

"Laszacko, this better be life or death news, or I am going to put you on a fingerprint project for the next year," Clutch groaned, rolling out of bed.

"Listen, my sister just called to report that a person has left the villa where Maria was living. She could not determine if the person was a man or woman, but the person was limping and carrying a cane. The person also had two small carry-on flight bags and one gym bag. As the person was getting into the car, the person stated something like *con them* to the taxi driver." Colleen waited.

"Crap," Clutch sighed. "I will bet you Maria is on the run again. I need to move on this information. Can I meet you in thirty minutes at the sheriff's office?"

"Sure," Colleen muttered. "I will see you there." She hung up the phone. Now her brain was firing on all cylinders. Questions suddenly started forming: Was this person Maria? Why would she be limping? What's up with the cane, and what the heck is the term *con them*? She rushed to get dressed, threw on her lightweight jacket, grabbed her mug of ice water, and left.

Colleen arrived just as Clutch, O'Neill, and Johnson were driving into their parking spots. All mumbled something like "good morning," or something to that effect, before heading into the sheriff's department. Within minutes, Clutch had coffee going, O'Neill was on his phone to some FBI Special Unit team commander, and Johnson was on the phone to the night commander at the Fusion Center. *Well, this is nice*, Colleen thought to herself. *Here I am sitting here with nothing to do but wait on these guys!* The phone conversations continued for five more minutes. O'Neill was talking to someone about slips and seals. Clutch was trying to find a Vietnamese translator. Johnson was trying to find out what flights were leaving the Tan Son Nhat airport in the next two hours. The conversations all ended simultaneously. Everyone looked at each other.

Then Clutch asked each person, "What are your agencies doing?" O'Neill stated that a few field operators in the Saigon area were heading to the villa. Their purpose was twofold: to kidnap Maria if she was there and, if not, to confirm that Maria had been there using forensic tools. Johnson stated that his men were looking into all flights leaving the Tan Son Nhat airport in the next two hours. If possible, his government contacts would tap into the video cameras in the airport and at all boarding areas.

"Laszacko, what do you have to contribute to this mess?" Clutch asked.

"Nothing. I am only reporting what my sister just observed about one hour ago," she stated.

"OK," said Clutch. "Our first priority is to figure out what the term *con them* means in Vietnamese. My friend who is a Vietnam citizen will be here in ten minutes, so maybe he can help us figure out what this term means. O'Neill, how long before your team can be at Maria's villa?"

O'Neill looked at his watch, then at the ceiling, and stated, "I expect they will arrive in thirty minutes."

Clutch then turned to Johnson. "What did you find out about flights leaving the Tan Son Nhat airport?"

Johnson replied, "There are fifteen flights leaving in the

next two hours. While all of the rest are going somewhere else in the world, two flights are going to New Orleans and Miami."

Clutch paused before asking Johnson one more question: "Are any of these flights going to Mexico City?"

Johnson stated, "Wait one minute," and he called the commander at the Fusion Center. "There is one flight leaving this airport, flying to Mexico City, in forty-five minutes."

Clutch asked, "Can your friends tap into the video system in the boarding area of the flight going to Mexico City?"

"Sure, just let me make another call." Within minutes the video cameras operating in the Saigon airport were visible on three big-screen televisions. Everyone was glued to them.

"Laszacko, what did your sister tell you about the person leaving this villa? You know the person's size; they were walking with a limp and carrying a cane. Is that right?" Clutch asked.

"Yes, that's right," Colleen said. All four were watching the screens when Clutch and O'Neill spotted an overweight woman limping down an aisle toward the Emirates flight going to Mexico City. Johnson was on the phone to his friend at some government agency, asking if the video showing the limping woman could be enhanced. Within seconds, the woman's face and physical appearance appeared on one of the televisions. Everyone noticed that the woman was very short, her hair was dark, very long, and her build was heavy.

Clutch asked, "O'Neill, do you think this could be Maria?"

"I want Johnson to have this woman's face put into our facial recognition system. Let's see what the machines tell us," O'Neill said. Johnson had all of these things happening as soon as O'Neill spoke.

Clutch then asked Johnson, "Is there any way we can watch this woman board the flight to Mexico City?"

"Hang on," Johnson said, "I'm working on it."

As they all continued to watch, the video tracked the woman right to the boarding gate. *Amazing*, Colleen thought to herself, *Big Brother is definitely watching us!*

"Laszacko!"

Colleen jumped. "Yes, sir!"

"Can you call your sister again and have her describe how tall she thinks this person was?"

"I can do that, and I might suggest we see if we can get access to the hotel's video, which may have caught enough of this scene to give us more evidence," Colleen stated.

"Great idea, Laszacko. Get on it now."

Immediately, Colleen left the conference room and called Kris. She answered on the first ring. "Sista, fill me in. What is happening?"

"Kris, we are going into hyperspace trying to follow up on the information you gave me an hour ago. Can you ask Paul if his security cameras may have caught any part of this person leaving the villa tonight?"

"Sure, hang on," Kris began shaking Paul. "Paul, Paul! Wake up—Colleen needs to talk to you," Kris was gentle but firm in getting Paul awake.

"OK, OK, Hon, I'm up. What is going on?" Paul asked.

"Colleen is on the phone, and she needs to know if your security cameras may have picked up this person I told you about leaving the villa."

"Let me get up and see if I can locate the video camera that might show this," Paul told Kris as he left the bedroom. Kris then talked to Colleen for the next five minutes. During this time, Colleen filled Kris in on what had happened and where the hunt for Maria was switching to now. Colleen also explained to Kris how Big Brother can watch you from thousands of miles away.

"That is some scary stuff," Kris said.

"Yes, it is, but in this case, Maria needs to be caught and brought to justice. I am glad we have the abilities and type of equipment to tap into the computers of an airport thousands of miles away," Colleen said.

Paul called on the hotel room phone. When Kris picked it up, Paul said that the cameras had picked up the person leaving the villa as well as the taxi company name and license plate. Colleen heard all of this and told both of them to stay on the line. After Colleen put them both on hold, she contacted Eric Johnson and reconnected both Paul and Kris so they could talk with him. Eric gave Paul some information, and, within minutes, the hotel video tape was appearing on another television. Everyone stopped and looked at this video. Just like Kris had described, there was a person walking with a limp, carrying a cane, and leaving the villa with two small carry-on bags and a gym bag. The video had no audio, but the taxi's license plate was visible, and the video showed the approximate height of the person.

"Great work," Eric told Paul and Kris. "We will take it from here. Thanks again and please contact us if you observe anything else occurring in or around the villa." Eric hung up. He then phoned his commander to give him the license plate on the taxi, and, within seconds, the name of the cab company and the driver's picture appeared on another screen. O'Neill jumped into the conversation and contacted his operators in Saigon with this information.

Dispatch called back to the conference room, announcing that a Mr. Hao was there in the lobby. Clutch left the room to get Mr. Hao. He brought him into the undersheriff's office and got him a cup of coffee. After a few sips, Clutch asked Mr. Hao, "I need your help. One of our most wanted suspects may have been seen leaving a villa in Vung Tau, Vietnam. This possible suspect was heard saying the words *con them* to the taxi driver as they left the area. Does that term mean anything to you?"

Mr. Hao asked Clutch, "Are you sure the person said *con them*?"

"Yes, it sounded like that, but again—the person hearing this was about ten feet away."

Hao took another sip of coffee, then scratched his head and told Clutch, "I believe the words this person heard were *con thuyen*. It sounds like *con them* in English, but in Vietnamese, it is pronounced *con thueem*."

"What does that term mean?" Clutch asked.

"It means *boat* in Vietnamese."

"Boat," Clutch said. "Boat. Does that mean there are boats in the area?"

Mr. Hao replied, "You stated that this person was living in Vung Tau, Vietnam?"

"Yes, we think this person may have been living in this area in a small villa for a period of time," Clutch stated.

"Vung Tau is a very busy beach resort area. There are a number of commercial and private boats in the area. Also, there are a number of ferries used in the city. Several are new speed boat ferries connecting Vung Tau to Saigon. If you think this person is your suspect, he or she could take the ferry to the Tan Son Nhat International Airport."

"Thank you, Mr. Hao. I was wondering if you could stay here for another five minutes or so? I need to have one of my colleagues talk to you," Clutch asked.

"No problem," Hao stated and continued sipping his coffee.

O'Neill and Clutch returned to the office where Mr. Hao was sitting. Introductions were made; then O'Neill asked Mr. Hao if he could tell us how long it takes the ferry to go from Vung Tau to the landing in Ho Chi Minh City, then to the airport.

Hao scratched his head, then stated, "I think about ninety minutes on the ferry, then about fifteen minutes to the airport." O'Neill asked Hao if he had ever taken this ferry trip.

"Yes, I have taken it with my family. It was a fast way to get to the airport without the hassles of country driving." O'Neill then shook Mr. Hao's hand and left. Clutch did the same thing and escorted Mr. Hao out.

Laszacko was thinking about something else while all of this other investigative activity was going on. She remembered that Maria Hernandez was about forty-six to forty-nine years old. She had a terrific figure, probably weighed maybe 110 pounds, was 5'3" inches tall, and her hair was black and long. She looked again at the frozen picture of this overweight, older looking woman. The woman looked obese, walked with a limp, and her hair was short. Even using all of this facial recognition software, neither the computer nor anyone else looking at this woman would believe that this was Maria, but she was not sure.

Doaks arrived in the conference room with coffee and a doughnut. He was getting caught up by O'Neill when he too looked at the frozen picture of this person getting on an airplane to Mexico City. "That's Maria!" he shouted.

"What the h - -l are you talking about?" Clutch and O'Neill responded.

"That is Maria! I am sure of it!" Doaks again yelled.

"How do you know that is Maria?" Clutch asked.

"Because twenty years ago, I was working as a detective investigating a huge embezzlement case at a restaurant called the Hut. Our prime suspect was a woman, in her twenties, extremely pretty, and extremely cunning. You have seen a picture of Maria Hernandez and know how pretty she is. On that day, our search warrant teams were in place, ready to execute a warrant on the Hut to seize its financial records. Everyone at the scene had a picture of Maria Hernandez. We executed the warrant and found part of the financial records we needed, but Maria was never found at the scene. During the debriefing on this warrant search, three of our deputies commented on seeing an older woman leaving the Hut, walking with a slight limp, and carrying a cane. The woman was overweight and was leaving in a hurry. Then a few years later, I was again looking for Maria as a possible murder suspect. Our department was given a tip on a specific location where Maria was staying. I had my SWAT team in place, and just as we were going into the location, I remember an overweight older woman, walking with a limp, carrying a cane, and leaving the area in a small car. Given what I have observed during this hunt for Maria the murder suspect, then given what the deputies described, I am betting you $1,000 that this person is Maria, using the same disguise she used twenty years ago!"

"Dang," Clutch said. "Let's go with Doaks' information and track where this woman goes."

Doaks then sat back, ate the last of his doughnut, and sipped his coffee. *This is going to be a great day*, he thought. Little did he know that in hours, his day would be wrecked with the discovery of body parts lying on several beaches near the Hut.

Chapter Fourteen:

Parts of Salsa and Maria's Escape

September 28, 2021

I walked into my office at 7:15 a.m. I was just about to sit down when Doaks appeared.

"Moving a little slow?" Doaks croaked.

"No, I stopped to get some coffee at the new coffee house off the highway and decided to walk the beach near the Hut before coming into work," I said.

"Well, Hood, sit down and let me update you on Maria's latest actions." For the next twenty minutes, Doaks gave me a rundown on what had been happening over the past three hours.

"Interesting stuff," I told Doaks, "but do you think Maria would still use that type of disguise to get out of Vietnam?"

"Hood, remember, crooks always repeat their crime patterns, and the same goes with their disguises. I am betting Maria was that person we saw leaving the villa in Vung Tau and is now heading to Mexico City," Doaks bellowed.

Just then dispatch called me on the intercom. "Detective Hood, please pick up line four," the dispatcher said. I told Doaks to stay put and picked up the phone. Deputy Morgan was on the phone. "Yes, this is Detective Hood," I said.

"Detective Hood, Morgan here. I need you and Sgt. Doaks to come over to Sombrero Beach as soon as possible. I believe I have a number of what looks like body parts washed up along the beach. I need you and Sgt. Doaks to verify if these parts are human or not." Morgan waited.

I rolled my eyes and then pointed at Doaks. "Get ready! We now have possible body parts washing up on Sombrero Beach," I told him. Then I told Morgan, "Please secure the scene; we are enroute."

Doaks and I took separate cars to the beach. As we were driving, dispatch asked for one of us to head toward Bahia Honda State Park Beach. People there had just called 911 to report body parts appearing to wash up on this beach also. *Great*, I thought, *body parts on two beaches. This is going to be a very long day.* I contacted Doaks and told him I would take the Sombrero Beach call and asked him if he could take the Bahia Honda call. Doaks agreed and headed that way.

I don't remember what time I told dispatch I had arrived on scene, but there were no beachgoers on the beach. In fact, it was desolate. Morgan had secured a very large crime scene and came over to me. "Detective Hood, I think I got all of the pieces inside my protected crime tape," Morgan stated.

"Looks good," I said. "Let's see what you found," I told Morgan as we headed toward the crime scene tape. *Crud, crud, and more crud*, I thought to myself. There on the beach were a number of fingers, toes, an ankle, and a possible ear. All of these parts appeared shrunken and shriveled. It appeared to me that they had been in the ocean for a period of time. I counted about ten individual body parts spread over a twenty-five-foot area along the north side of the beach. I was just about to begin my crime scene documentation when I heard dispatch call me again. "Hood here," I responded.

Dispatch stated, "We are now receiving numerous 911 calls from people finding more body parts at Coco Plum Beach, Loggerhead Beach, and Curry Hammock State Park Beach." Dispatch then asked me to switch to another radio frequency. I answered them on Channel 3, and they asked, "How should we handle these multiple calls on body parts washing up along the beaches in these other locations?"

I replied, "You need to check with Sgt. Doaks first. In the meantime, please direct all available patrol units to each location to secure the scenes. Also, if we do not have enough patrol officers on duty, please contact the Chief Deputy about these expanding crime scenes." I clicked off my radio and continued processing the scene. For the next thirty minutes, I photographed, sketched, and diagrammed each of the individual body parts located on this beach. I was able to get some evidence markers from my car, but I only had nine evidence flags, so I was one short. *Dang*, I thought to myself, *I need to get restocked on these things.* I was just about to complete my crime scene documentation when I saw something rolling in the surf in front of me. I waited until the tide brought the object onto the beach, then I looked at it again. *Crud*, I said to myself. This object looked like part of a thigh. I waited until the body part had sunk into the sand, then I proceeded to take more pictures and document this new piece of evidence. I was just about to put all of my evidence into my trunk when I wondered about finding a cooler to preserve all of these body parts. I turned around just as a man was coming down to the shoreline carrying two coolers. I walked over to him, introduced myself as a police officer, and asked him if I could use one of his coolers.

"Why do you need a cooler?" the man asked.

"I have about eleven pieces of evidence. It appears that all of this evidence is human, and I need to get everything refrigerated as soon as possible."

The man made a face. "Yuck! Are you telling me that all of those yellow flags in the sand, and that big plastic flag near your car, are human body parts?"

"Yes, sir. Now could I borrow one of your coolers?" I asked.

The man put both coolers down, turned green, and then puked. "Sorry," he said, "I am not used to seeing human body parts on my beach." I told him I understood, and he gave me one of his coolers, partially filling it with ice from his other cooler. "Hey," he asked, "can I get my cooler back?"

"Sure," I told him. "Here is my business card. Just call

me tomorrow, and I will return it to your place." The man left and, unfortunately, I heard him throwing up again as he headed toward his car.

I managed to get all of the body parts into the cooler and had enough ice to cover them. I called Dr. Spock. I told him that I had eleven body parts; Doaks expected more because our department was getting calls on more possible body parts washing up on three other beaches. Spock told me to have all of the officers bring the body parts to his morgue and he would put them in a freezer as soon as possible. I was just about to thank him when Doaks called me on the radio. I told Spock I would do that, then hung up.

"Hood, switch to Channel 3," Doaks ordered me.

"OK," I said and asked him what he wanted.

"Hood, I have twelve body parts here. How many do you have there?" he asked.

"I have eleven here."

"What do you think we should do to preserve all of this evidence?" Doaks asked. I told him that Spock wanted all of these body parts taken over to the morgue ASAP. Doaks agreed.

I radioed that I was enroute to the morgue, and the Chief Deputy and Clutch asked me to go to Channel 3. I switched my radio to Channel 3. Clutch asked me to look at one of the larger pieces of evidence I had in my car. I told him I would have to pull over first. After I pulled off the road, I picked out the thigh I just took off Sombrero Beach. Clutch had me take the thigh out of the plastic container and closely look at the cut mark(s). I wondered what the heck Clutch was thinking, but I did what I was told.

Clutch then asked, "Does the cut on the skin and bone appear to be one cut or several?" I thought to myself, *This is nuts. I am about to get sick handling this thigh, and now I am closely examining the cut mark(s) on it?* I was about to say something stupid when Clutch specifically asked me again to look at the cut mark(s) on the bone—was it a clean cut done once?

"Yes," I said, looking at the thigh and its bone, "one cut through the skin, muscle, and bone."

"OK," Clutch said, "get that body part over to the morgue; then go to the other locations to supervise the handling of all the other body parts."

"Yes, sir," I stated, then switched back to our main dispatch channel. *Crud*, I thought, *this is turning into a nightmare for our department!*

I reached the morgue and brought in my cooler of body parts. Dr. Spock was supervising the placement of all this evidence. I left my cooler with his assistant and headed back to one of the other beach crime scenes.

Doaks met me and grabbed me by the arm. "Hood, do you believe this? All of these body parts? This is nuts! In thirty years of police work, I have never, ever seen this much destruction on a human," Doaks sighed.

"Yep, this is nuts," I said. "I wonder how many humans are involved with all of these pieces floating along our beaches?"

Doaks shook his head. "I have never seen anything like

this before and, after today, I do *not* want to handle another case like this again. I am getting sick." I had to contain my immediate reaction: Doaks getting sick? I was about to leave the lobby area when Doaks asked, "Have you gone over to the other crime scenes?"

"Not yet," I said. "I just brought in my evidence from the Sombrero Beach scene." Doaks then asked me to go and supervise the other beach crime scenes while he was going to talk to Dr. Spock.

As I was heading out the back door, Spock yelled at me: "Hood, don't leave without taking these coolers with you! They are filled with ice, so you can put all of the body parts collected at these crime scenes in the coolers and document them properly!" he ordered. I picked up the coolers, left the morgue, and headed toward the next crime scene—Curry Hammock State Park.

Clutch entered the morgue five minutes after I left. He went over to Dr. Spock and asked him to put one of the body parts under a computerized scanning microscope. Then he directed Spock over to a computer in the lab. There he pulled up an earlier crime scene he had investigated with several photos of body parts. Clutch was adjusting the focus on a picture of a finger and a toe when Spock told him his microscope had focused on the cut mark on each item. Clutch then put both screens from the microscope and the computer screen together and looked at the mark made on each piece of evidence. "It appears to be a similar if not a perfect match. I believe we are looking at the work of the Tongs gang here. They are ruthless, and they mean what they say when they tell their rivals 'If you cross us, we will chop you up into little pieces!'" Clutch said. After a short pause, he continued. "Dr. Spock, with your permission, I would like to have the department's plane fly into Marathon and take several pieces of this new evidence back to our crime lab in Miami. Is that ok?"

"Of course," Spock stammered. He couldn't believe what he had just seen and now heard: instant analysis, albeit a day, on pieces of evidence left at a crime scene. Within an hour the DPS aircraft had landed, taken the pieces of evidence on board, and was flying them back to the crime lab for analysis.

Clutch was just about to leave when Doaks came over. "Assistant Director, how is the hunt for Maria going? Any luck?" Doaks inquired.

"We believe she is now heading to Dubai International Airport, then on to Mexico City. Unfortunately, we did not get enough information from the airport cameras. Thanks for asking. Also, thanks for your help in describing how Maria has used this type of disguise in prior cases." Clutch shook Doaks' hand and left.

Chapter Fifteen:

Identification of Body Parts, and Where Is Maria?

September 29, 2021

The start of another day. *Lord, please do not start this day like yesterday*, I thought to myself, looking skyward.

Doaks came in around 7:45 a.m. "Hood, let's meet in my office in ten minutes. I want to discuss and debrief on yesterday's body parts investigations."

"Sure," I told him and headed toward the coffee machine in our conference room. Ten minutes later, Doaks and I were just about to begin our debriefing when Clutch and O'Neill came into the area.

"Hood, you and Doaks need to hear this from O'Neill," Clutch stated. Like little kids, we both sat back in our chairs in Doaks' office and listened as O'Neill delivered the information.

"The pieces of human parts floating onto our various

beaches have been confirmed by our criminal lab. They are from the body of Salsa Rodriquez, Maria's daughter. Unfortunately, we have no leads on who killed her, nor do we have any indication that it was definitely the Tongs gang from Vietnam. Our forensic experts have verified that the body parts were cut by the same type of weapon—a Vietnam sword called *Trurong Dao*. This sword is very sharp and very strong. Our agency has seen a similar display by the Tongs in San Francisco where we found a number of body parts floating along the beaches in the San Francisco Bay. We were able to match the cut mark left on Salsa's body to those left on two rival gang members in San Francisco. Our intelligence gang unit was not aware that the Tongs were operating in the Florida Keys; however, given this incident, they are redirecting their resources into the Keys now." O'Neill stated that he was finished and asked us if we had any questions.

Doaks asked, "Aren't the Tongs part of the Snake Gang in the Golden Triangle area?"

O'Neill reacted strangely. "How do you know about the Snake Gang in the Golden Triangle area?"

Doaks replied, "A few years ago, I began my own personal study on upcoming gangs involved in drug trafficking in the United States. The Snake Gang, particularly the Tongs, were mentioned as the next drug gang taking over the Mexican cartel action in the United States." Doaks stopped and looked at O'Neill, who was clapping his hands.

"Good work, Doaks! Sometimes for an old cop, you still

amaze me." *Crap*, I thought, rolling my eyes again, *why is O'Neill feeding this guy's ego?*

Clutch then interrupted my train of thought and asked, "What do you think will be Maria's reaction to the murder of her daughter?" Doaks was still feeling his ego when I told both Clutch and O'Neill my thoughts.

"Maria will come back and seek vengeance for her daughter's murder. I believe she will be returning here sooner rather than later, and we will have a war with a high body count before this issue is resolved," I told them. Doaks unexpectedly excused himself and left the conference room.

"Where is Doaks going?" Clutch asked. O'Neill looked at me, then told Clutch, "My bet is the restroom." I agreed, and we both shook our heads. Clutch then looked at me and asked, "Why do you believe Maria is coming back here ASAP, and why a war?"

"I have been studying Maria Hernandez for a long time. I find her to be ruthless toward anyone who crosses her or Salsa. Salsa meant the world to Maria. Given her possible involvement in seven homicides over two decades, I would be preparing our law enforcement community for a war. We all experienced her battle expertise at the warrant raid at the Hut. Doaks and I saw her handiwork firsthand in attacking us and a protective witness at two safe houses and on a Coast Guard Cutter. We need to gear up. Maria Hernandez is coming, and the body count will be high," I concluded.

Clutch looked at O'Neill, then said, "We need to get

Johnson involved, and I want to have a conference with our task force in fifteen minutes. O'Neill, please see that your director is notified because I want him involved in our task force meeting." Clutch then left.

O'Neill hesitated. He looked at me and asked, "Would you like to have dinner tonight?"

I was a bit taken aback, given the gravity of the situation we had just been discussing. "Let's put a hold on that request for a while. I need to see where we are following our task force meeting," I said.

"No problem; good idea." Then O'Neill left. *Dang*, I thought to myself, *O'Neill seems to be interested in me beyond our task force relationship. I'm not sure I'm interested in him.* Then I remembered that I need to chill out sometimes when looking at relationship potentials. *Let's see what tomorrow brings*, I told myself, then went back to my office.

Meanwhile in Dubai—7,913 miles away from Key Marathon—Maria was meeting with her favorite arms dealer. About twenty minutes earlier, she had received a call from one of her confidants in Key West stating that Salsa had been murdered and cut up into little pieces by the Tongs. Maria swore she would kill all of the Tongs gang in the Keys and beyond for murdering her daughter. But right now she needed to concentrate on purchasing enough weaponry to eliminate the Tongs gang—and anyone else involved in Salsa's murder. When Maria was done, she had arranged for enough arms and other explosive devices to be delivered to a unique charter jet she had just booked three hours prior. Maria thanked her friend, then left the store. Within minutes Maria was back in her hotel suite, changing clothes and taking on another passport name and appearance. For her next flight to Mexico City, she was going to be Valencia Gomez.

Valencia was fifty, with long gray hair, tall, and slightly overweight. Her flight to Mexico City was going to take off in five hours. She left her reservation in place, but she had also booked a private jet back to Key Marathon. This jet was unique in that it was built with stealth technology. It was the property of a royal prince who needed to get in and out of certain countries undetected. Maria had paid top dollar for this aircraft, but she did not care. She needed to sneak back into Marathon, and this jet was her way to return. Maria decided to take a nap before heading to the private airport adjacent to the Dubai International Airport. She had decided that she must return to Key Marathon as soon as possible. The death of Salsa was too hard—but there was no time to grieve now. Instead she would seek revenge. Vengeance is what she would bring with her on her chartered private jet.

The task force meeting started at 10:30 a.m. All of the task force members were there, plus a number of other high-level government VIPs listening and watching via Zoom. Clutch spent a few seconds introducing the director of the FBI, the director of homeland security, the DPS director, and two other VIPs Johnson had insisted on inviting. Clutch then started our discussion with two areas the task force needed to determine:

- What is Maria Hernandez doing in Dubai?
- Where does Intel think Maria is located now?

For the next thirty minutes, everyone with the rank of director and above discussed their opinions and their answers to these two questions.

Doaks began to fall asleep. I kicked him under the table, and he jolted awake. "Dang, Hood, why did you wake me up? These guys know all the answers to these questions. You and I are peons in this intellectual quagmire discussion—no one cares a rip about you and me," he whispered.

Just then Clutch halted the discussion and asked Doaks and me what our opinions were. Doaks turned and looked at me, then said, "Detective Hood, why don't you answer the Assistant Director's questions for both of us?"

I stared daggers at Doaks, then whispered in his left ear that I was going to beat his hind parts. I turned and addressed the task force: "I believe Maria, or whatever name she is using now, will be here in Key Marathon in the next twenty-four to forty-eight hours. Salsa meant the world to her. She will get her revenge, and it will be a bloody war. I would suggest our intel community focus on any connections Maria may have in Dubai. Dubai is known for its access to weapons, and I think Maria went to Dubai to obtain enough weapons to eliminate the Tongs and anyone else involved in Salsa's murder. I also believe our law enforcement community along with our intel community needs to locate Maria's associates still living in the Keys. Also, in my opinion, Maria can afford to rent a private jet to fly from Dubai to the Keys. We need to figure out where a private jet could land to offload weapons and explosives and where Maria is going to be staying when she returns."

When I finished, the director of the FBI and one of the VIPs Johnson had invited asked, "How did you come up with these ideas?"

I took another deep breath, glared at Doaks, then said, "Sgt. Doaks and I experienced the wrath of Maria when she was attempting to kill a witness in our protective custody a few weeks ago. Her intel was excellent since it was coming from one of our own commanders. She attacked two safe houses and a Coast Guard Cutter trying to kill our witness. Her army was well equipped with weapons and explosives. I know what she is capable of, and I expect she will have more weapons and explosives when she arrives here. Again, I would focus our resources on locating as many of Maria's gang members still has living in the Keys. If we focus on Maria's connection in Dubai, we should be able to determine what she is bringing to this fight and where she can offload it and be prepared to stop her before this war begins." I shut up.

Clutch was hushed. In fact, the entire task force looked at me, then at Clutch. He said, "I agree with Hood. Now let's do what she is telling us to do." No one from the directors to the VIPs said a word. All simply agreed and left the meeting.

Clutch called me outside the conference room. "Hood, sometimes you amaze me. That assessment of yours was spot on. Good job in getting the entire intel community in the country on your side. You were impressive."

"Clutch, thanks, but I don't do well with compliments. Let's just catch this b - -h and put her away for life. She killed and injured a lot of cops I knew, and I believe we need to figure out where she is going and stop her there. If not, I think we will have a war—a huge war—on our hands, and innocent civilians could be injured or killed." I turned to go.

"Where are you going?" Clutch asked.

"I am going to our jail," I stated. "I want to talk to Salsa's husband, or ex-husband. I think he may have some information most helpful in getting us some answers to our two questions." I turned and walked back to my desk. Then I contacted the jail commander and asked to speak to the pod supervisor where Jairo Rodriquez was being held.

Chapter Sixteen:

Somewhere over the Atlantic Ocean

September 30, 2021

The jet had just taken off from the Miami Executive Airport. It had been a long flight from Dubai to Miami. Next stop was a prepared runway located on an abandoned missile site on Key Largo, Florida. The jet was not seen by any radar. Why? Because it was flying fifty feet above the ocean. The transponder was off, and the stealth covering on the jet was working. Over the past few weeks, Maria had been busy organizing her undetected return to the Keys. She paused for a minute, then reflected on what had happened over the past eight days.

Salsa had contacted her on September 20. She was in trouble with her drug dealer. A new group had taken over the drug trafficking in the Keys. This group was known as the Tongs. Salsa had decided to start her own drug trade without getting permission from the Tongs. That had cost Salsa five million dollars; then it cost her the most important thing: her life! When the Tongs visited Maria in Vung Tau, she knew Salsa was dead. On September 27, early in the morning, Patron, Maria's assistant, contacted her, and told her that Salsa was dead. This call set into motion a plan Maria had been working on for weeks—the return to Key Marathon.

After Patron had called her, she contacted her second cousin A. Q. "A. Q." were the initials for Antonio Quinns, director of the Key Largo Hammock Botanical State Park. Now the park had been renamed the Dagny Johnson Key Largo Hammock Botanical State Park. It was a former missile site known as *HM 40*. A few days ago, A.Q. declared an emergency and closed the park for the next three days. During this time he initiated a runway reconstruction plan on an old highway: State Route 4. The runway project needed 6,000 feet for Maria's private jet to land. A. Q. had about two days to get this runway ready to receive Maria's jet. That meant he needed at least thirty workers ready to cut trees, fill potholes and road cracks with concrete, create a temporary lighting system, and have several vehicles in place sometime between 1:00 a.m. and 3:00 a.m. on September 30. A.Q. had already contacted El Jefe, another assistant in Maria's organization, to make sure his men were ready to make this happen. Maria named her plan *Plan A. Plan A is not complete, though*, she thought. *I need to find a place to store my equipment, and I need a place to stay.* Patron had suggested two locations for Maria. The equipment could be stored in an abandoned mansion located at the end of Coco Plum Drive. This place was 15,000 square feet and had been in some type of legal battle with the City of Marathon over the past nine months. Maria's new living arrangement was a VRBO located two houses south of Salsa's residence. It was booked for six months.

Then the pilot let her know that her destination was on the right and that they would be landing in five minutes.

At 2:15 a.m. Maria's special private jet landed on old State Route 4. A Q. and El Jefe had done an excellent job in lighting up the runway. The pilot had enough space to land, turn the plane around, and unload equipment. There were several vehicles for the equipment and two SUVs for Maria and her team. After thirty minutes, the jet left the runway at 2:45 a.m. and disappeared into the dark Florida sky.

Maria told everyone at the site, "Thank you. Now let's get moving." The vans and the two SUVs left the area and headed north to Key Marathon. Maria was smiling in the back seat, thinking, *It's good to be home again. Salsa, I will avenge your death and create a blood bath never seen before in the Keys!* By 4:00 a.m. the equipment and vans were hidden at the mansion. Maria was sleeping in her VRBO while El Jefe and Patron had enough guards, security cameras, and perimeter protection in place to catch anyone breaching any of these locations.

I was planning to go over my notes from the interview I had with Jairo Rodriquez, Salsa's husband. Jairo was not surprised when I told him about Salsa's death and finding her body parts on several beaches. "If I had found her with another man while I was traveling, I would have done the same thing, only she would have suffered a lot more than me just killing her," he commented. I reread my interview notes, trying desperately to get some type of intel on Maria's next moves. Jairo felt that Maria would return very soon and avenge Salsa's death. He, like me, thought there would be a war. In fact, he believed that Maria would take this fight outside the Keys into any location where the Tongs were operating. Jairo did not have any other specific intelligence to assist our task force.

I left the jail, went back to headquarters, and started to type up my notes. Doaks came into my office holding a cup of coffee and grumbling.

"Hood, we have nothing, nothing, on finding that b - - h, and we don't have a clue on the Tongs. This whole thing is nuts—totally nuts! What do you think?" he asked me.

I hesitated before answering. "Um," I told him, "I think you and I need to do our own thing now. The task force is too big and doesn't know our turf like we do, so let's begin to work our informants, see what we can find, and show the task force how good detectives work in Marathon."

"D - - n good idea, Hood. Let's go to Sally's and eat breakfast. We can work out our plan of action," he chortled as he left my office. "See you there in fifteen," then he was gone. *Crud, there goes another twenty bucks of mine feeding Doaks. I am going to ask the sheriff for a food budget just to keep Doaks happy.* Off I went, but my brain was hitting overdrive thinking about what our next moves would be. Little did I know, Maria was here and getting ready to attack.

Doaks finished his big breakfast in five minutes, had three cups of coffee, then looked at me. "You on a diet?" he asked. I had decided to save money and ordered the early bird special: one egg, toast, and coffee—five dollars. Doaks then asked, "What are your thoughts about locating the Tongs and where they might be?"

"Garcia and Lopez are meeting us here in two minutes. These gang guys seem to know everything about any gangs operating in the Keys. I thought we could begin with them and see where it takes us later today," I told him. Both men arrived and joined us in our booth. Garcia, a seasoned gang officer, spoke first.

"The Tongs are a very secret gang, and the only way into this gang is by birth. The only intel I have comes from my police contacts in Key West and Miami. Both departments have found bodies chopped up in their areas over the past weeks. The Tongs are ruthless. They take over an area, rule it with force and murder, and let their reputation scare away any competition. My Key West contact believes they were working out of a Vietnamese restaurant in the downtown area called the Sister's Noodle House. This place is located near the Gulf on a major highway. My contact said this was an educated guess since no one had been able to conduct any type of surveillance on this place recently."

Lopez then jumped into the conversation. "The Tongs are a new gang getting into the U.S. drug trade. We have found them to be active on the west coast in the San Francisco and

San Diego areas. They probably have been here longer than we know, but I would guess several of our known drug dealers have been visited by them. I suggest you start there and see what you can find," he suggested.

"Great ideas," Doaks said. "We will get started on this now, and could we keep you in the loop in case we need help and more ideas in the future?"

"Sure," both officers said, then left.

Great, I thought to myself, *Doaks and I really don't have a clue about this Tongs gang and given what we just learned, we are on our own trying to find more information on them.*

Doaks was still scratching his balding head, then said, "Crap, we have nothing—and they were not a lot of help. We are back to square one, Hood. What are your thoughts?"

"The same as yours. I think we need to hit up a few of our friendly drug dealers or informants to see what they can tell us. I believe the Tongs are so intimidating that they will not talk to us, but with a little persuasion perhaps they will give us some information," I suggested. I paid the bill, and we left. First stop, our informant Diego's friend, Spike.

Spike hung around J. J.'s Dog House. He was there when Doaks and I arrived. I saw him leave the lobby and quickly disappear into the back of the place. Doaks caught him coming out the back exit and had a little talk with him. Spike was 5' tall, but with his hair spiked up, he was closer to 5'6" tall. Spike was not in a good mood. Doaks and I noticed that Spike was missing a few of his hair spikes today.

"What happened to your spikes?" Doaks asked.

"Nothing. Just leave me alone and get the h - -l out of here," he grimaced at us.

"Spike, you have three outstanding traffic warrants, and you missed your court appearance last Friday. Do you know what that means?" I asked him.

"Kiss off, Hood! I know what that means. So what?" he spat.

"So what?" I asked. "Perhaps a few days in jail with special conditions would help your attitude toward Doaks and me," I related to him.

"Listen, I ain't talking to you, now or forever, got that?" he yelled.

"The Tongs been around lately?" Doaks asked.

"Who? What are you talking about?" he bluffed.

"Spike, we can do this one of two ways. You and Doaks and I take a car ride someplace isolated, and you tell us everything you know and have been doing under the direction of the Tongs. Or I take you to jail, put you into isolation for a few days, and let you rot there," I threatened. Spike began to twitch—first a little, then a lot. He was sweating putty balls, and he was looking all around the area. We were at the back of J. J.'s facing a high concrete fence and lots of homes and trailers. No one was around, and no one was watching us, so I again asked, "What do you want to do?"

Spike then whispered to me, "Listen, the Tongs are bad, bad news. I heard what they did to this girl—Salsa. Then a friend of mine told me that his friend disappeared two days ago, and I think he will be chopped up next. I cannot be seen with you at all. So how do you want to do this—smuggle me into a car and leave, or what?"

I had Spike under my control when Doaks arrived at the back of J. J.'s. I opened the rear door and threw Spike into the back seat, telling him to lie down and stay quiet. Doaks then left the area, and I followed about three minutes later. We decided to go to one of the safe house locations. We both knew the area was deserted and there were no neighbors. Doaks got there first; I arrived two minutes later. Under the shade of a big coconut tree, Spike, Doaks, and I talked.

Spike started babbling, talking about one hundred miles an hour. His speech was nervous, and he was very jerky. I finally grabbed him by his arms and shook him. "Spike, settle down! We are here, and no one else can see us or find us. Now slow down and tell us what has happened to you." For the next thirty minutes, Spike spoke nonstop about what had happened to the drug trade in the Keys since the Tongs arrived. He told us that the Tongs arrived at his residence one day and had a one-way conversation with him. They told him that everything he sells will come through them. Anything they give him is what he gets—no negotiation, nothing. If he didn't like it, the Tongs would kill him, then chop up his body. Word had travelled up and down the Keys about this new gang and how they had already killed three dealers in the Keys and had no problem killing anyone who didn't cooperate.

"How do you meet them? How do you get their drugs to sell? What about the money? How do you get it back to them?" These and several more questions I asked Spike. Spike got really nervous again, and he was jumpy. I grabbed him and shook him again. "You're OK! We got you! Just answer my questions," I said. Several deep breaths later, Spike told us how his interactions with the Tongs worked.

"They contact me and tell me a location to meet them. I go, they give me my drugs, then check me for any wires, guns, or other metal things with a wand device. My cell phone doesn't work wherever they tell me to go; I thought that was different. Once I make my sales and collect my money, they call me and tell me where to meet them for the exchange. Again, I go there; I am searched, wanded, and my cell phone dies. None of the locations are the same. Each time the drug pickup and the money exchange are at different places. So far, all have been on Marathon. That's all I can give you, sorry."

Well, I thought, *that is better information than we had at breakfast.*

Doaks looked at me, then at Spike. "OK, Spike, where do you want me to drop you off?"

"Just leave me here. I think I know where I am. Let me get back to the highway later. You just leave. OK?"

"One other thing, Spike. I want to meet you again in two days—same place, same time behind J. J.'s OK?" I told him.

"Why? Why do you want to put me out there so the Tongs can kill me?" he cried.

"Listen, I hear you loud and clear. Remember I picked up Salsa's body parts yesterday, so I know what the Tongs can do. We need to deal with them, right now, and you are the only person with firsthand information. You stay alive, and we will protect your back—ok?" I said. Spike shrugged, then said OK. He walked away from us, probably terrified.

Doaks looked at me and said, "Let's go to McDonald's for coffee—I'll buy!"

Wow, Doaks is going to buy. What is going on today?

Chapter Seventeen:

Tongs, Maria, and War

October 7, 2021

Over the past week, our lives (Doaks and mine) had been too quiet. No reported homicides, no found body parts, and nothing from the task force. That all changed today. First, our department began to get some unusual reports that a woman seen in Marathon, on Point Key, resembled our suspect, Maria Hernandez. Second, our department had been notified by several people in Key Largo about some mysterious noises coming from what may have been a small landing strip on Key Largo. These noises occurred about one week ago, in the middle of the night. Finally, Rhonda—a woman I interviewed on a prior case who lived next door to Salsa's house—contacted me. She said she was positive she had seen Maria, or at least a woman looking like Maria, living two doors south of Salsa's address over the past three days.

Doaks came into my office, looked at me, and sat down.

"What the heck is going on? One week of peace, now all of this! What are your thoughts on these recent sightings of Maria?"

I too was a little taken aback by all of these so-called Maria sightings. In my mind, I asked myself one question: why would Maria come back to the exact same location where she knows she is wanted? I was still thinking about all of this information when O'Neill barged into my office.

"Hood, I think Maria Hernandez is now living on Point Key."

"Really," I said. "Where are you getting this information from?"

O'Neill promptly answered, "From a variety of people, several living in VRBOs on the same street that Salsa's house is located. And, recently, one of her neighbors—a woman named Rhonda who has lived next door to Salsa's house—has reported to me personally that she is sure Maria is back."

"What are you doing about these sightings?" I asked him.

"Nothing right now. Our task force is still dealing with the information we gathered from Maria's villa in Vung Tau, Vietnam. I can say that we have proved that Maria Hernandez was living there for a period of time, but now she's gone," O'Neill sighed.

"So, what are you doing about these recent reported sightings?" I asked again.

"Clutch is floating up a drone in the next hour. The drone can be programmed to circle the area where these Maria sightings are occurring. Clutch seems to think that by using this drone, we can verify if this woman looks like Maria or not," he said.

"Does Clutch have a game plan if the drone sights this mystery woman?" I asked.

"Yes, he does. If the woman looks like Maria, then he will move in a surveillance team to watch the house," O'Neill said.

"Great, and in the meantime, what would you like Doaks and me to do?" I inquired.

"Keep working on the Tongs. Find out more information on their headquarters and anything about their drug dealings, and continue pushing your friend, Spike," O'Neill said. Then he left, but not before giving me a wink. Doaks was not sitting in the right position to see the wink, but I wondered about it.

O'Neill and I had had a real date, last Friday. No one knew about it, and I wanted to keep it that way. O'Neill was a really nice guy away from the station and out of his role with the FBI. I have to admit that I had a great time. O'Neill was the perfect gentleman. He met me at a very nice restaurant outside of Key Marathon. Treated me to a great dinner and left me with the impression that he would like to start dating. I, on the other hand, had not quite made that jump from one date to dating. I was still thinking about that when Doaks snapped his fingers at me.

"Hood, what the heck are you daydreaming about!" he yelled.

"Nothing, why?" I yelled back. Doaks was getting a kick out of watching me now.

"Hood, if I am wrong, please tell me. Are you seeing O'Neill?" he asked sheepishly.

"Shut up, Doaks!" I yelled, then said, "no way. You know I do *not* date anyone I work with. Now, can we get back on track? Where is Spike now, and did you call your friend at Key West PD to find out if he had any intel on the possible locations of the Tongs?" I fired back.

Doaks ignored my questions, jumped up, said goodbye, and left my office. After he left I was able to refocus on the next steps in the investigation.

I was sitting at my desk when my phone rang. "Hello, Detective Hood, may I help you?" I recited.

"Hood, get over here now!" Doaks barked at me and hung up. *Nice, Doaks is really beginning to piss me off*, I thought to myself as I grabbed my laptop. I got to Doaks' office and saw that he was talking to someone on the phone. I sat down in his office chair and listened. It appeared that Doaks was on the phone with a detective from another agency. He was furiously writing down words and partial sentences as he listened to this person talk. Doaks then put the person on hold, took a deep breath, and began to talk to me. He was talking nonstop, waving his hands, totally absorbed in his one-sided conversation, and oblivious to me. His antics went on for three minutes. Eventually he stopped, shook his head, and flipped me off. *Nice*, I thought, *Doaks finally realizes he is not making sense to me*. Doaks then showed me his open palm and telling me to wait another minute.

He continued talking to this man, now identified as a lieutenant from San Diego PD. He hit the speaker button, then said, "Lt. Nguyen, I apologize for cutting you off. My partner just came in as we were talking about the Tongs in San Diego, and I wanted to bring her up to speed on the information you just told me." Next he asked the lieutenant if he would please talk to our task force commander, Assistant Director Clutch. The lieutenant agreed, and Doaks put him on hold.

Then Doaks ordered me to run down to the conference room, find Clutch, and get him on this phone line. *What the heck? Why am I the go-to person now*, I asked myself as I hustled down the hallway to the conference room to find Clutch. I arrived to find Clutch on the phone, but he was hanging up. I rounded the corner into his office.

"What's up, Hood?" he asked. Why are you running or at least walking at a quick pace?"

"Clutch," I said, "Doaks is on the phone with a commander from San Diego PD. This person appears to have a lot of critical information about the Tongs, and he would like to share it with you. Can you pick up line three and talk to him now?" Immediately Clutch hit the flashing button, introduced himself, and they began a three-way conversation. In the meantime, I headed out of the conference room to the coffee pot. Given these conversations, I was going to need a lot more caffeine in my body this morning.

At 11:30 a.m. I was just about to get lunch when O'Neill, Clutch, and Doaks entered my office. I laughed to myself,

Here we go, the Three Stooges are here, and the circus is about to begin. (*Dang, I'm bad*, I tell myself, but looking at the three of them, the Three Stooges were the first image that came to mind.) All three crowded into my office and began to talk at once. I laughed at them, signaled the "time out" sign with my hands, and asked Clutch, "Would you like to go first?"

O'Neill and Doaks looked away for a second, and then Clutch said, "Thank you, Hood. We need to bring you up to speed on the latest information we just received from San Diego PD." For the next twenty minutes, with only minor interruptions from Doaks and O'Neill, Clutch educated me on the actions of the Tongs in California and in Key West. I learned a lot and was about to ask a question when Johnson came running into my office.

He stopped and in a loud voice said, "There has been a massive explosion and shootout in Key West. The target was a restaurant called 'the Sister's Noodle House.' According to the Key West PD, there are bodies in the highway and the Gulf and a number of vehicles and buildings on fire. Key West PD is requesting our assistance there ASAP, so we all need to go now." With that, everyone left my office and headed to their cars. The entire task force evacuated the conference room and within sixty seconds, everyone had piled into their own patrol vehicles, turned on their red lights and sirens, and made a mass exit toward Key West.

Doaks jumped into my vehicle and said, "Wow! This looks like a three-ring circus."

"Yes, it does—why are we *all* going down there?" I asked.

"I don't know, but when Clutch, Johnson, and O'Neill all run out of your office into their own vehicles, I believe we are dealing with some serious s - -t," Doaks said. I agreed. So now there were ten unmarked police vehicles running Code 3 down the only highway in the Keys heading to Key West to the location of the Sister's Noodle House restaurant.

We all arrived about the same time. The crime scene was massive. The entire area must have been at least one mile long and about one mile wide. There were charred cars, bodies, and boats and hundreds of looky-loos surrounding the crime scene. Key West PD and a dozen DPS officers were doing their best to keep the crowd from entering the crime scene.

I looked at Doaks. "Holy crap!" I yelled, "this is a total mess!" He shook his head, and we headed out to the command post. We made it to the first perimeter. There we were checked by a uniformed DPS officer before we were allowed to enter the next perimeter. There again we were checked, then signed into the area by another DPS officer and permitted to enter the command post.

Inside the command post was organized chaos. The incident commander was a DPS captain. He had his incident command operations in place. Each area was assigned into a small booth in a large command trailer. O'Neill and Clutch saw us and motioned for us to come over to their location. Neither of them had an office; they shared a desk with a placard reading "Special Task Force, Federal and State Operations." We sat down at the desk just in time to hear the incident commander ask O'Neill and Clutch to join him in a small conference room adjacent to the bathroom. O'Neill and Clutch left, ordering us to stay at this location. We agreed and listened to the activities going on inside the command post. I was very impressed at how all of the cops from all of these different agencies were investigating this massive crime scene and dealing with the ongoing emergencies occurring outside.

As we listened, we picked up some information. First, there appeared to be several more bodies found adjacent to the blown-up restaurant and in the marina adjacent to this site. In addition, there appeared to be a dozen bodies strewn along the highway near this restaurant. We continued listening as the fire coordinator and the emergency response coordinators stated that there were no survivors. The emergency room at the only hospital in Key West was told to stand down and get ready to receive a number of dead bodies.

Doaks then poked me. "I wonder what Dr. Spock would be doing if he were in charge?" Just then Dr. Spock walked into the command post and headed directly to the incident commander's location. He was stopped by another ranking DPS officer and asked for identification. Spock showed him his credentials and was escorted into the private closed conference room where the incident commander was. The door closed, and Doaks jabbed me again. "I wonder what their conversation is about?"

"Listen, Doaks," I told him, "touch me one more time,

and I will smack you. Got it?"

Doaks made a face, then apologized. Inside I was going nuts—enough sitting around doing nothing. I wanted to go out and help with the crime scene investigation. I wanted to assist cops in photographing, documenting, or identifying and collecting evidence, but there I was still sitting! Just on cue, the small conference room door opened and Clutch started barking orders for me and Doaks.

"Doaks, can you please go to the restaurant area to assist these officers in their investigation? I want you looking for some indication of a major explosive device. Hood, can you go to the section of the highway two blocks south to assist Nurse Laszacko with her investigation on the cars and bodies left in this area?" Immediately we left and reported to our assigned locations.

Four hours later, Laszacko and I completed our initial investigation on thirty bodies. Most of the bodies were inside the fifteen burned-out vehicles we processed along this highway. The smell of burning human flesh was awful. Both Laszacko and I were wearing face masks and had a large amount of Vick's VapoRub under our noses. Still the smell was awful. There were no survivors—most of the bodies were badly burned. Our preliminary investigation showed that each vehicle had thirty or more bullet holes plus two or three large holes in each car. We looked at the diameter of each hole and thought that maybe an RPG (rocket propelled grenade) type weapon was used. This was something we both wanted to pursue in our follow-up investigations.

We also saw that many of the victims inside these vehicles were shot numerous times and had died before they were burned. Laszacko told me that she would be sending all of her information to the DPS crime lab immediately, and hopefully she could determine the cause of death on most of these bodies prior to the autopsies in the morning.

Dr. Spock stopped by to talk with Nurse Laszacko about putting a temporary morgue at the hospital. She agreed that we needed to get that started; she also suggested that we contact most of the forensic investigators working in DPS and ask them to come to Key West as soon as possible to help in processing this crime scene. Spock then left, and Doaks arrived at our crime scene. He waved at Laszacko, then told me to step over to my vehicle. He was parked outside the crime scene, and the air conditioning was working great.

"Dang, it's humid out there. I need a complete change of clothes," I told him.

"I agree with you," he said, "but let's talk about this crime scene. Have you ever seen, or ever heard of, a crime scene with this many bodies and this amount of destruction?"

I thought about it, then answered, "No!"

Doaks got quiet, looked around, and then looked at me. "I think this is the work of Maria Hernandez."

"Maria? Do you think she's the one who did all of this?" I asked him.

Doaks looked around again, then said, "I believe that

Maria is going to continue her revenge on the Tongs until she is convinced she has wiped them all out. I think this is just the beginning as she eradicates the Tongs in the Keys. And I am very worried what her next target will be."

I looked at Doaks again, "You're serious about this being the work of Maria?"

"Yes, I have seen her handiwork when she was a prime suspect in the murder of a teenager who allegedly tried to rape Salsa in high school. I knew what she was capable of back then, and, given the amount of time she has had to plan her revenge, I believe we will see another war zone in the next few days."

I looked at Doaks, then I looked outside. Seeing this amount of death and destruction was a first in my life. "Doaks, if you're right, we need to get this information to Clutch, because we are going to have to put our task force into overdrive and get more resources down here as soon as possible," I told him. Sitting back in my car, thanking God that the air conditioning was working, I thought, *God help us if this turns out to be the work of Maria Hernandez. If so, we are in for a long, long war—one we don't have any intel on yet.*

Chapter Eighteen:
More Crime Scenes—Has Maria Returned?

October 10, 2021

The investigation of the crime scene in Key West lasted several days. The evidence collection on the bodies and vehicles was very time-consuming. Ten more forensic investigators from DPS and several from Miami PD assisted our task force in collecting the evidence and processing what we found. A temporary morgue was set up outside the Key West Hospital. There were sixty bodies in it; more were expected. None had been identified yet. Doaks and I worked several crime scenes. The bodies just seemed to keep coming, appearing under vehicles or in trees or on top of buildings—the worst part was the explosion in the restaurant. Here, whatever type of bomb was used had caused body parts to be located almost a quarter mile away. Our work was long, tiresome, and tedious, but we had our rules for handling evidence and did our jobs correctly. Finally, on day three, Clutch ordered Doaks and me back to Marathon to follow up with our confidential informant (CI), Spike.

A few days later, we met Spike behind J. J.'s Dog House. He was very jumpy and began asking us lots of questions. "What the h - -l happened in Key West?" was his first question.

Doaks looked at me, and I asked Spike, "What have you heard?"

"I heard there was a huge explosion and a huge shootout."

"What do you know about this?" I asked.

Spike looked away and then smiled. "I heard the Tongs got their butts kicked big time and I heard there is some woman who has promised to kill all of the Tongs in the Keys, then in the rest of our country!" he exclaimed.

"Really?" Doaks shook his head. "You have been hearing this from whom?"

Spike kicked his feet on the asphalt, shook his head, scratched his chin, and said, "Word on the street is some woman has gone nuts because her daughter was killed by the Tongs. She has a lot of muscle and enough weapons to eliminate the Tongs and their influence here in the Keys. The woman has a name I can't remember, but it has something to do with a witch in Spanish. She has promised to avenge her daughter's death and has put out contracts on any known Tongs gang members anywhere in the Keys," Spike said.

Doaks looked at Spike and said, "The name of a witch in Spanish is *bruja*. Is that the name you heard?"

Spike stared at Doaks; I looked at Doaks questioningly.

"Yes!" Spike jumped up and down. "That is the name I heard."

I looked at Doaks again. "Where are you getting this information?" Doaks just laughed and pointed to his head. Then I asked Spike, "So where are you picking up this chatter from?"

"My friend, Pablo, has a friend called Patron. According to Pablo, Patron welcomed back his old crime boss a few weeks ago. This boss is a female, and she is ruthless. I have been told she just returned from a long vacation, and she has plans to take back all of the drug trafficking in the Keys and beyond."

"Do you have any information or description on this woman?" Doaks asked.

"No, and what if I did? Why would I give you any information?" Spike smirked.

Doaks looked at me and scratched his chin. Then with one swift move, he grabbed Spike by the throat, lifted him off the ground, and whispered in his ear, "Listen a - - e! Don't get smart with us because I will rip your tonsils out and cram them down your throat, got it?"

Spike wet himself and then, with his eyes bugging out, grabbed Doaks' right hand and croaked, "OK, OK!" Doaks released his right hand from Spike's throat area and let Spike's feet hit the ground. I was impressed with Doaks' actions. I made a note to commend him on this move later, but now we had more information to find out. For the next five minutes, Spike did all of the talking. He told us about a change in the Tongs' way of doing business. He also stated that last night he was supposed to meet the Tongs at this location, but they never appeared. Today, he was expecting to get directions on where to pick up his next drug shipment, but no one from the Tongs had contacted him yet. Spike then looked at Doaks and asked, "Am I missing something?"

Doaks replied "There was a huge explosion in a Vietnam restaurant in Key West five days ago, and there was a massive shootout on the highway where this restaurant was located. It appears that most of the victims were either members of the Tongs or their associates. I don't know about your contacts, but I believe for the time being that the Tongs are out of the drug business for a while."

Spike looked at Doaks, then at me. "You're s - - g me," he stammered.

"No, you dumb a- - s. This is no B.S., and we need your help," Doaks said, putting his hand on Spike's shoulders.

"Crap," Spike said, knocking Doaks' hand off his shoulder. "I will give you one thing," he said.

"OK," I replied, then grabbed his right hand, spun him around, and cuffed him in nanoseconds.

"What the h - -l?" he yelled, then tried to run away. Doaks tripped him and he fell on the asphalt drive, banging his head and getting some road rash on his right cheek.

"OK, Spike, enough games—and quit your crappy excuses," Doaks yelled as he picked him up off the pavement.

"OK! OK!" Spike cried. "What do you want me to do?"

Doaks looked at me, then I told Spike, "You and I are

now becoming best friends. From now on, when you hear anything from anyone, you will call either Doaks or me. Got it?" I asked.

"Yeah," he stammered. Then Doaks took the cuffs off Spike's wrists and told him the new rules of our game. Spike was to become our instant informant, or he would be taken to jail, placed in solitary confinement, and given a special label in the jail population—*snitch*. Spike settled down and agreed to help us. Doaks let him go, and he slinked away.

Doaks and I looked at each other. "McDonalds for coffee?" he asked.

"Sure, and you're buying," I laughed and headed toward my car.

The ballistics results on some of the bodies and cars slowly trickled into the task force. Clutch initially thought the bodies appeared to be shot by automatic weapons. The DPS and FBI crime labs' preliminary reports indicated that the weapons used in this attack were a PKM, machine pistol, or FNM3Ps. These weapons were the latest models in machine guns/pistols, and only a few countries had them available on the black market. Clutch and O'Neill started asking Johnson for intel on these weapons.

"Where could you buy these weapons today?" Clutch asked. Johnson was scrambling for some current information on the weapons.

He replied, "My best guess would be somewhere in the Middle East. A very rich country would have access to these weapons and a few more interesting pieces of explosive devices."

"Explosive devices," Clutch said.

O'Neill jumped in and asked Johnson, "You mean explosive devices that make the size of those large holes we found in several of the vehicles?"

"Yes," Johnson nodded as he pulled up details on his computer. He continued looking at his screen until he found some very specific information. O'Neill then went to his computer and typed in the initials *RPG-7V2*.

"Dang," O'Neill said. "This RPG-7V2 can kick some serious butt. No wonder the holes in these vehicles were so big!" Clutch looked over and saw a picture of the weapon. O'Neill asked, "Clutch, did you say our suspect, Maria, may have stopped in Dubai?"

"Yes," he nodded. "My sources say Dubai is one area where the largest arms dealers in the world are in business. Do you want to bet Maria spent some time there, purchasing these weapons, bombs, or other devices?"

"Is there any way we can verify your weapons information and perhaps tap into some video locations around these suspected arms dealers?" Clutch asked.

Johnson got a little nervous and started rubbing his hands together. He turned to Clutch and O'Neill and said, "Listen—I am cashing in favors and signing IOUs by the dozen working here. For me to get that type of information is way, way, *way* above my paygrade. Sorry I can't get you what you want," he sighed, shaking his head.

O'Neill stood up, thanked Johnson, and told Clutch, "I may have another way to get some information on weapons, video, and some other interesting things in Dubai. Can you give me fifteen minutes?"

"Sure," Clutch agreed as O'Neill left the conference room and headed out into the hallway. Clutch and Johnson looked at each other and wondered who he was contacting or what agency he was now talking to.

"I'll bet you twenty dollars he is on the phone with the CIA," Johnson chuckled.

"No," Clutch replied, "I think he is on the phone with some of his out-of-the-country people, working his friends in Special Operations." They laughed. They really did not know too much about O'Neill, but they both knew that his contacts were well known outside the circles of the FBI.

Fifteen minutes later, O'Neill came bouncing into the office, looked at Clutch and Johnson, then told Johnson, "Go to this website." Johnson immediately typed the website into his laptop. O'Neill told him to slide over and let him handle the rest. Within three minutes, O'Neill had pulled up several video feeds around the city of Dubai. He had found two specific locations inside this video surveillance area where he believed the task force could possibly learn about Maria's actions in Dubai.

I popped into the conference room and was met with instant stares and hushing noises from the three men. I rolled my eyes, then laughing to myself, whispered, "OK, what did I walk in on?"

Clutch motioned me to come over to the chair next to him while Johnson and O'Neill focused on the images on the computer screen. Five minutes later, I saw Maria Hernandez leaving an old building. "That's her!" I yelled.

"OK," Clutch and O'Neill whispered. "Let me freeze the picture and see if I can see some type of address," O'Neill said. Clutch and Johnson had both slid their chairs back from the computer and began to whisper to one another, totally ignoring me.

Nice, I thought, *I am no longer considered part of this exclusive boys' club—I guess I'll sit here for another five seconds, then leave.* I was about ready to leave when O'Neill told me to come over and look at this woman again. I slid my chair next to his and again exclaimed, "That is Maria Hernandez!"

O'Neill then asked Johnson to take a screenshot and run it through the facial recognition system. In the meantime, O'Neill had Clutch write down an address: Al Khail Rd. E44, #3 Hatta Rd. After Clutch wrote down the address, O'Neill told everyone to huddle. He whispered, "This is the last known location of an arms dealer, Omar Abdulla Malik, wanted in several countries. Israel and Germany have several agencies trying to locate this man because of the weapons and destruction he has brought to both countries. If Maria contacted him or any of his associates, we are in for another round of incidents involving massive death and destruction." O'Neill copied and pasted the screenshot and sent it out to three email addresses, all of which were outside our country.

"Great," Clutch sighed. "I can hardly wait to find out what she'll be doing next."

Johnson was on the phone with someone from the Fusion Center, and O'Neill was on the phone with someone in Washington, D.C. Time for me to leave. But O'Neill grabbed my arm and told me to please hold up for a minute; I did. He escorted me out of the conference room into a deserted hallway.

"Can we go out on another date, tomorrow night?" he asked.

"Ah," I stuttered, "Let me check on some things and get back to you later today, OK?"

"Sure," he said and told me to not say a word to anyone on what I had just observed in our conference room. I nodded my head and walked toward my office. *Dang. Who is this O'Neill guy, and who does he know,* I thought. I sat down at my desk and was reaching for a bottle of water when Doaks arrived.

"Hood, you will not believe what I am about to tell you," he stammered as he plopped into my guest chair.

"OK, what information do you want to share with me that I will not believe?" I responded.

"Well... " then Doaks stopped. "Do you know what I am about to share with you? Did you hear this from one of your friends on patrol? Am I the last one to know about this incident report?"

"Listen, Doaks," I said, shaking my head. "Just tell me what information has you all excited?"

"OK," he said, "but please let me know if you know about this stuff!" Over the next five minutes, Doaks related a very unusual story about a possible jet, landing on an abandoned Nike missile center on Key Largo, then leaving.

"Where in the world did you hear this one?" I asked. Doaks stated that his friend living on Key Largo was up late a few nights earlier and swore he heard a small private jet engine whining as it approached Key Largo. He heard the sound but did *not* see anything. About thirty minutes later, he heard the jet whining to take off when he saw the exhaust from twin engines on a small private jet leaving Key Largo. He looked at his watch and saw it was 2:45 a.m. Doaks' friend wanted him to know in case we were tracking an illegal shipment of drugs into the Keys. Doaks thanked him for the information and told him we would be checking it out. "So, what do you think about this information?" he asked.

"Did you check out any reports mentioning anything about a jet landing on Key Largo on that date?" I asked.

"No," Doaks said, "but let me look at our daily radio log reports and our field information (FI) cards to see if there was anything noted in patrol that day."

"What day are we talking about?" I inquired. Doaks scratched his head, looked up for divine guidance, then said, "I am not sure what day—perhaps September 30 or Oct. 1."

I looked at Doaks, shook my head, and asked, "Did you do any research about a Nike Missile Site on Key Largo?"

Doaks looked at me. "What am I, the information guide for the Keys now?"

I again shook my head and asked, "Do you remember anyone talking about a Nike Missile Base on Key Largo in the past twenty or so years that you've lived here?"

Doaks looked at me again with that blank stare. "I don't remember anything about a Nike Base on any of the Keys except Key West, but I may be wrong."

I told him to sit still and let me work. Within a couple minutes, I found there was a Nike Base located on Key Largo and that it had had a landing strip at one time. The base was in service from June 1965 until June 1979 and was part of the U.S. air defense system. The base closed and was later given to the state of Florida and converted into a state park. Today the park is known as the Dagny Johnson Key Largo Hammock Botanical State Park.

"Crap," Doaks stared at me, shaking his balding head. "Why didn't I think of that?"

"Doaks, this is called an *iPhone*. It has Google, and if you would have taken five minutes to type in the phrase 'Nike Base Key Largo,' in nanoseconds you would have found this information. When are you going to walk into this century?"

Doaks got a sheepish looking smirk on his face. "OK, OK, Hood, you're right. Maybe next year I will be able to afford a used iPhone, but not now!"

I looked at him and asked, "What do you want to do, given this information?"

There was no immediate answer from Doaks, but finally he said, "Let's take a ride."

"A ride to where, and why now?" I protested.

"Shut up, Rookie, let's go." Doaks and I left my office, jumped in my patrol vehicle, and headed to Key Largo to Dagny Johnson Park.

We arrived at the park in twenty minutes. No one was at the entry gate, so I drove in. After driving around for a minute or two, I spotted an old section of road on the west side of the island. I had to wind my way onto the road; then I was immediately blocked by a steel yard arm. Doaks looked at me.

"Does that road go on to the other side of the beach?"

"I don't know, but let's jump the gate and see what's out there," I said. We did and began walking on an old roadway. The road had several sections—very old and weathered—but as Doaks and I continued walking, we saw several disturbing things. First, the trees and bushes in one area had been trimmed back. Next, many areas of the old road that had cracks or potholes had been recently filled with asphalt or concrete. Finally, as I was walking toward the ocean, I saw what appeared to be tire tracks made by a plane landing on a runway.

Doaks ambled over to me and asked, "This road looks like there was some recent repair work done on it. These trimmed-back trees and bushes look recent as well as these tire tracks. "Why would someone do this now?"

I asked, "How far do you think this roadway goes?"

"I don't know, but—"

I was interrupted by a person in a park ranger uniform yelling at us, waving her arms, and heading in our direction.

"What are you doing here? This area is off limits! Why did you ignore the No Trespassing signs?"

I was ready to pull out my badge and ID, but Doaks had pulled his badge from his belt, identified the two of us as police detectives, and asked the woman what occurred here. The woman was taken aback and did not answer us immediately.

She then said, "I apologize for interrogating you, but this area is designated as off limits to park visitors." She then stated that she did not know anything about the trees and bushes being cut, nor did she know anything about the old roadway being patched.

I asked, "Has anyone reported any unusual activity involving this park over the past two weeks or so?"

The woman looked puzzled, then answered, "I don't think so, but can I get back to you later?"

Doaks then asked, "One more thing: who is in charge of the park now?"

"Our director is Park Superintendent A. Q., Mr. Antonio Quinns," she stated, "but he's been on vacation for the past few weeks." *Interesting*, I thought. I asked her if we could drive our car out onto the roadway and take some measurements and perhaps collect some evidence? The woman became very interested. "Why do you want to drive your car onto this old, deserted roadway and collect evidence?" she asked. Doaks then told the woman about his friend's story involving a jet landing here. The woman looked at Doaks and said, "Interesting story. I too have heard a number of our neighbors talking about some jet noise or something sounding like a jet landing in the area a few days ago, then taking off. Is that why you want to bring your car out here and take some tire track samples?" she asked.

"Yes," Doaks said before making a request. "We would like to walk the entire length of this roadway and see if there may be any evidence of a jet landing here then taking off." The woman said OK, went back to the gate, and unlocked it.

I told Doaks, "You keep looking around. I will go and get the car." I left and brought the car to the edge of the old road. Doaks in the meantime went walking along the old road. He stopped about one hundred yards in front of me. He was bending down, looking at something in the sand, when I arrived. "What do you see?" I asked.

"I found a bullet buried under the sand here. It looks like a 7.62 round, but I wouldn't know for sure until I got back to our crime lab."

"Interesting. Do you see anything else?"

"Not yet, but you take the other side of the roadway, and let's walk out to the ocean." Doaks and I slowly walked along the old road. Over the next twenty minutes, I found several interesting things in the sand, as did Doaks. In fact, we both found what we believed to be several tire tracks left on both sides of the road; then we found more live bullets under a palm tree. These bullets looked similar to the one Doaks found. Doaks then looked at me and said, "Hood, I think we're looking at a drop zone here. These tire tracks, these bullets, and now these markings on the roadway indicate to me we may have had a jet land here and offload some weapons and other things."

Great, I said to myself. *More weapons, and only the good Lord knows what else.* I then went to the tire markings on the roadway, scraped some material off the road, and placed it into an evidence bag.

"Hood, let's go back to HQ and see what we can find after we examine this evidence at our lab." I agreed, then I did one more thing: I drove my vehicle the entire length of the roadway starting from the first indication of clearing the trees and bushes until it ended at the ocean. My odometer indicated that I had driven about 1.3 miles. *Wow, that is a long distance. I wonder how much runway a private jet needs to land and take off?*

That question and several others would be answered the next day. Doaks and I left the park and headed back to HQ.

Chapter Nineteen:

The *Isabella?* Evidence and War

October 12, 2021

Todd Hood received a phone call at 8:00 a.m. The caller was Sam Burton. Sam was considered a coin collector professional in recognizing and cleaning ancient coins. He was also a member of the American Numismatic Association—the only coin collection organization recognized by the U.S. Congress and the Professional Numismatists Guild. Over the past weeks, Sam had been cleaning the object Todd and Shane had discovered in the Atlantic Ocean off Duck Key. The object was found at a depth of one hundred feet.

Sam told Todd, "The object you had taken off the ocean floor contained some interesting things. First, there were a number of gold and silver coins. The coins were from the 1700s. They were different sizes and had different amounts of gold or silver in them. In addition to the coins, I have cleaned off another piece of this object and found an ornate dagger. The dagger had several encased jewels. I was not sure if these were diamonds or emeralds without more extensive cleaning. I also found another item that appeared to be some type of letter opener. It was made of solid gold and had some initials on it. I think the initials may be E.D. The lettering appears to be in Spanish." Sam said that he needed more time to check another source to make sure his interpretation of the letters was correct.

"These items need more cleaning and more handiwork," Sam said. "Do you want me to proceed with more cleaning on both items?"

Todd replied, "Yes—please go ahead, and let's see what else we can find on these two things." Todd asked about the estimated value of the coins and other items Sam had worked on so far.

Sam's estimate on the value of these coins—and the two other items—was around $500,000.

"Holy crap!" Todd shouted "$500,000?"

"Yes," Sam explained. "I believe the total value of your find could actually go higher. But again, I still have some more cleanup work to do on the other two items."

"Can you keep all of these things in a secure place while I contact my lawyer?" Todd asked.

"Sure. I'll continue working on these other things and await your phone call after you talk to your lawyer. By the way, I'm glad you're getting a lawyer involved. The laws surrounding sunken treasure, particularly in Florida, are very tricky. Your lawyer needs to be trained in this field, and you should expect to pay a lot of money to retain him or her."

"Thanks," Todd replied. "I will be in touch soon." He hung up the phone, sank back into his lounge chair, and repeated his thoughts out loud. "Holy crap, I cannot believe that piece of rusted metal stuff turned out to be worth half a million dollars. I have to call Shane!"

Shane was working on a new type of jet propulsion engine when Todd called him at work. He hesitated to answer the phone because he was at his desk in the middle of a project involving a new type of engine, but when he saw who it was, he stopped typing on his computer and took the call. "Uncle Todd, how are you?"

"Shane! I am fine and getting better as you will find out after I tell you some news." Todd continued, "Do you remember the man we took the rusty object to? The one we found in the ocean last month? Well, he called me today to report what he found. He's cleaned away all of the rust, and we now have several gold and silver coins, a dagger encased with some type of jewels—diamonds or emeralds—and what appears to be a solid gold letter opener. The projected total value of our find is estimated to be $500,000."

There was a long, silent pause on Shane's end. Then: "$500,000?"

"Yes!" Todd said, "and it may have more value once Sam removes some other stuff off the jewels and the letter opener."

"What do you think we should do next?" Shane asked.

"I think I am going to call a buddy of mine who is an attorney and ask him for his advice. The laws on finding sunken treasure in Florida are interesting, and I want to make sure prior to us notifying anyone outside our families that we are legally set to move forward to claim ownership and to make sure our find is properly claimed by you and me." Todd paused. "Shane, are you OK with this?"

Shane shook his head and looked outside his window. *How could a piece of rusted material turn out to be worth this much money?*

"Shane," Todd asked, "are you OK with what I told you?"

Shane, still shaking his head, looked around and finally answered his uncle. "Yes, let's do this. Please keep me advised on how much I will owe you once you find the lawyer. Oh, one other thing—who knows about this?"

"Right now, just you and me. Molly is out shopping, and Katie is at work, so they have not been told."

"Can I tell Allie?" Shane asked.

"Of course, but I would suggest we not discuss this with anyone else yet—not until we have legal counsel and we can file the legal documents to officially possess what we found."

"Thanks, Uncle Todd. I'm still in shock, but I agree with your suggestions. Please keep me updated when you can, and thanks!" They hung up.

Doaks and I were in the crime lab when Clutch came running in.

"Where have you two been?" he bellowed. Doaks took the lead and told Clutch we had just come back from Key Largo, checking out another unusual lead in the case. We were trying to validate if a private jet may have landed on an abandoned road inside the Dagny Johnson Key Largo State Park. Clutch looked at Doaks. "Where in the world did you pick up that tip?" Doaks explained that a friend—a retired detective from his past—had contacted him a few days earlier, asking him if he had any information about a jet landing on the island, perhaps dropping off drugs. Clutch scratched his head and said, "So what did you find?" Doaks turned to me.

I was examining several live bullets found along the old state route road inside the park. I pointed out the pieces of evidence I was unpacking to put into another evidence container for processing. Clutch told me to wait a second; then he came over to look at the evidence.

He shook the container, then told us, "Let me take this now. I will get our DPS plane down here to verify if this tire track mark may be part of a jet wheel. Also, those several bullets? Let's add them along with the evidence here to see if there may be prints or any other type of evidence we can glean from them."

Doaks looked at me; then I gave all the documentation and evidence to Clutch.

"How long will it take for all of this to be completed?"

I asked.

"Not long. I will put a rush on the processing. Once the plane lands in Miami, I should get some results in an hour or less." Clutch then left the lab with the evidence while reaching for his cell phone.

I looked at Doaks. "So, what's next?"

Doaks got the call from Lt. Nguyen around 2:30 p.m. Nguyen was asking permission to join our task force to share his intel on the Tongs gang. Doaks put him on hold, then found Clutch. Clutch gave instant approval to have Nguyen join us in Marathon as soon as possible. In the meantime, Johnson was pulling out all the stops in gathering intel from a variety of sources on the Tongs gang.

Nguyen told Doaks to pick him up at the Key West Airport around 11:00 p.m. that night and asked Doaks to make reservations at a local hotel. Doaks told him not to get a car, said that he would cover his requests, and hung up.

Clutch and Johnson had begun to assemble the stacks of paperwork and intelligence information now pouring in from the Fusion Center. After studying the material over the next two hours, Clutch looked at Johnson. "Crud! These guys have a long history of extreme violence. We need to gear up our troops and get every cop ready for the onslaught coming soon." Shaking his head, Johnson agreed as he was scrambling to get some more international intel from three other sources.

Doaks and I entered the room and looked at both men.

"What are you guys doing?" I asked. Clutch took the lead and told us that they had been reviewing the updated intel on the Tongs gang and had learned a lot about the gang and their actions. Doaks jumped in, adding that Lt. Nguyen from the San Diego PD was arriving that night to join our task force. He was considered one of the leading experts on the Tongs and was coming to assist our investigation into the war we believed had started between the Tongs and Maria Hernandez's organization.

"Has anyone verified if Maria Hernandez is actually here in Key Marathon?" I inquired. All of the men looked at each other, shaking their heads.

Clutch said, "We have nothing concrete on her location here or anywhere else in the world, for that matter. We are just speculating on the after-effects of the mass shootout and the explosions down in Key West, given Maria's history using powerful weapons and explosives. Processing the evidence left on the bodies and cars at that crime scene, it appears that Maria's firepower shows what she is capable of when she is angry. I believe she is extremely pissed off and seeking massive revenge for Salsa's death. I also believe we need to follow up on finding where the h - -l she is and what the h - - l to expect in the future." Clutch looked at Johnson, who said nothing.

Then O'Neill burst into the room. "My contacts in Vietnam have just verified that Maria Hernandez was living in that small villa, and she has left. The pictures we saw in Dubai are of her, but we have nothing after that. I would like Doaks and Hood to start asking around about anyone who may have been associated with Maria's organization in the past decade. Let's pressure them into telling us if she is here on Marathon, in the Keys, or somewhere else. Oh, one other thing—my agency is now willing to put up some substantial money leading to any information on her whereabouts."

"Substantial money?" Doaks asked.

"Yes, substantial money in the form of Benjamins by the hundreds. Got it?" O'Neill said.

"Yeah, I got it, but how are we going to validate this information?" Doaks asked.

"We will introduce a new federal database we can now use on known or suspected gangs as well as terrorist groups and individuals," O'Neill replied. "This database is a new venture between several federal agencies trying to access numerous databases on known and possible gang and terror suspects in the world. The database went operational yesterday, and we should be able to access it today. Any information you pick up can be run through this system and, hopefully, in a few seconds or minutes, we can verify whether the information from your source is good or bad."

Johnson chimed in. "This new database has been operational in our fusion centers for the past six months, but this is the first time we are releasing access to a task force like ours."

I looked at Doaks and said to the group, "We will find out

if Maria is back. Just give us about twenty-four hours." Doaks and I left the conference room and headed out to my vehicle.

"Where are we going?" Doaks asked. "Back to the jail. My second stop is the state prison," I explained.

"Why the jail and the prison?" Doaks asked.

"Because I want to squeeze Jairo, Salsa's ex-husband, for some more contact information. Then I want to go to the state pen to squeeze Jose Hernandez about any contacts he might know who would help Maria," I told him. Doaks agreed, so we headed to the jail two miles away.

Jairo was brought to the jail's conference area five minutes after we arrived. He was very talkative that day. He, like many other convicts, alluded to having a lot of information but wanted us to promise him some type of reduction on his sentence. I had anticipated this move, which is why I had spoken to Mr. Moceri about a deal. Mr. Moceri stated that if Jairo gave us some valid information that led to the location or capture of Maria Hernandez, he would be willing to reduce Jairo's jail sentence.

Jairo got settled. "What do you want from me this time?"

I said, "We need to know anyone's name, street names, or any other information on people you know that were associated with Salsa or Maria."

Jairo scratched his head, then his right hand, then looked up at me. "What's in this for me?"

I shook my head and said, "Listen, do you like it in here? How's the food? How are the men? Have they gotten together with you yet?"

Jairo instantly turned red and stood up. "Shut up, b - -h!"
He turned to leave.

"If you have any—and I mean any—good information on
Maria friends, family, or associates, you need to sit your hind
parts in this chair, shut up, and listen to my deal!" I ordered.

Jairo was nearly to the exit door when he turned and
slowly walked back. He sat down and asked again, "OK, I'm
listening. What's in it for me?" He listened to Hood's proposal
and decided to talk for the next five minutes.

"Maria has a cousin whose name is A. Q. (Antonio
Quinns). He does something with the state park in Key Largo.
Also, Maria has one other person she has called her backup
go-to man: Patron. Patron has an associate called El Jefe. Both
of these individuals have been involved with Maria and Salsa
over the past years." Jairo paused. "So there is my information.
What's next?"

I looked at him and then at Doaks. "OK," I said. "We
need to check this out and see if this is good information or
more B.S. from you. If your information checks out, I will
contact Mr. Morceri, who will contact your lawyer and see
about a reduction in your sentence."

"S - -t, that could be weeks! I need to get out of here ASAP,
before I become one of the "friends" of one of the gang bosses
in here," Jairo whined.

"Shut up, Jairo," I raised my voice. "You got yourself
into this mess; you live with the consequences. I will validate

this information today, then make the call if and only if your information is good, got it?"

Jairo lowered his head, looked at the floor, and whispered, "OK."

One hour later, Doaks and I were inside one of our remote state prisons. There we met Jose Hernandez, Maria's husband. Jose looked bad. He was skinny and haggard and had a festering cut above his right eye. He entered the conference room, sat down, and flipped us both off.

"What do you b - -s want? Why are you here? Leave!"

Doaks grabbed Jose by the uniform, picked him up off the chair, and held him there with one hand. "Listen, you worthless piece of human s - -t. We came here to give you a shot at a reduction in your sentence, but since you continue to be an a - -e, the deal is off," Doaks said as he let Jose bounce off the chair, then onto the floor.

"Wait, wait!" he gasped. "What do you want from me?"

"Sit down and look at me." Turning to Jose, Doaks said, "Listen very carefully because I am only going to ask you once. What do you know about Patron, El Jefe, and A. Q.?"

Jose, scratching his head, looked around like a kid caught with his hand in the cookie jar. He whispered, "I know a lot about them."

"Good. Start talking or we walk," Doaks croaked.

A switch on Jose's mouth flipped, and, for the next fifteen minutes, he outlined the organizational structure he and Maria had set up over the past twenty years. Patron, nickname for

Jesus Cortez; El Jefe, nickname for Don Perdome; and A. Q., Antonio Quinns. Jose then told us what each man did in Maria's organization and where each one lived (as of six months ago). Once he finished, he turned and eyed Doaks. "OK, fat man, what do you have for me?"

Doaks was getting off his chair, but I grabbed his arm and said, "Let me handle this." I looked at Jose, got right into his personal space, and grabbed the back of his chair. He got nervous. I stared at him for a minute; then I shook his chair and told him to listen very carefully. I smiled and whispered, "First we will be checking out all of your information and, if you lied to us, I will see that the word *snitch* is your new prison nickname. If you have told us the truth, your public defense attorney will be getting a call from the state attorney's office about a possible reduction in your sentence here."

Jose looked at me, got up, and yelled, "Later, you pigs!" He flipped us off again and banged on the door to be escorted back to his cell. Doaks got up and was going toward him when I again grabbed his left hand.

"Cool it, Doaks. He is just trying to get you to do something stupid, so don't," I ordered.

Doaks took a deep breath, shook his shoulders, and looked at me. "Thanks, Rookie. I should learn to control my temper," he said. Then we left.

Chapter Twenty:

Tongs, Intel, and War

October 14, 2021

Lt. Nguyen arrived at the Key West International Airport at 11:00 p.m. Doaks recognized him as he entered the terminal. Doaks waved and Nguyen nodded and immediately came over. Introductions were made, and Doaks asked, "Any luggage?"

"No, I only take a carry-on during these visits because I only plan to be here about a week," he said. Doaks led Nguyen out into the parking area, and they headed up the Keys to Marathon. During the one-hour drive, Doaks and Nguyen exchanged information—mostly about their careers, with some talk about their divorces and their retirements. Both men had been cops in various law enforcement agencies over the past thirty years, and both had been involved in homicide squads. Nguyen talked about his new assignment creating a specialty squad on Asian gangs a few years ago.

They arrived at the Tranquility Bay Beach House Resort.

Doaks told Nguyen that he didn't need a car and that he would pick him up in the morning about 8:00 a.m. Doaks told him to take some time to adjust to the time change, dropped him off, and headed home.

At 9:00 a.m. on October 15, Clutch called a meeting of the task force for two reasons: first, to introduced Lt. Nguyen to the group; second, to allow Nguyen some time to give the task force updated intel on the Tongs gang and their history in the United States and the Golden Triangle of Vietnam, Cambodia, and Thailand. In addition to his briefing, Nguyen brought along some pictures of known gang members and their leaders. He explained how he had contacted Clutch for permission to fax all of these pictures to Dr. Spock to assist in identifying the bodies now in the morgue.

O'Neill stopped him for a second. "In your opinion, what's next? How will the Tongs react to this recent gun battle?"

Nguyen hesitated, then said, "In my opinion, I expect that the Tongs organization will send either the number two or three leader in their global organization to Key West. They will assess the damage, calculate the product loss, and request more personnel to take back any lost turf and regain control of the drug trade in the Keys."

Doaks then asked, "Do you anticipate any more gun battles or violence in the meantime?"

Nguyen answered Doaks with another picture—a gruesome picture—of a dozen individuals sliced up and hanging from a basement rafter. "This is how the Tongs take revenge on anyone taking over, or trying to take over, their territory," he cautioned.

I raised my hand. "Have you seen pictures of the Key West crime scene? The bullet holes in the cars, the extent of damage caused by significant explosive materials, and the use of possible RPGs?"

Nguyen nodded his head and stated, "I have seen the crime scene photos. I have never seen this type of firepower used in a gun battle in my career. Nor have I seen the amount of damage I saw to that restaurant and the surrounding buildings. I am concerned because you have no solid leads on suspects at this time. I believe that the Tongs realize this same issue and will come properly equipped to counterattack whomever was involved." Then he sat down, and Clutch took over the meeting.

Updates were given by all task force members. Doaks and I added our two cents' worth of intel on Patron, El Jefe, and A. Q. We told the task force we were in the process of checking out all of the information we had gotten from Jairo and Jose and should have an updated report within the hour. Clutch then asked Nyugen to spend some time with Johnson updating the intel on the Tongs at the fusion center.

Doaks and I left, went to my office, and started the computer using the "new database" for the task force. I got into the system and entered the names of each of these alleged suspects in Maria's organization. Within minutes, pictures, rap sheets, and NCIC, DPS, and other criminal records were illustrated, with updated addresses and other known safe locations, houses, and boats.

Doaks looked at me. "What now?"

"Let's pull all the records and information our department has on each of these suspects; then let's do an in-depth follow-up on any known associates. We need to know where these three guys are and what their plans are for the next week." We spent the next hour searching our records for information on these three suspects, finding known associates, family, friends, or anyone listed in past police reports.

Finally, at 12:00 noon, Doaks got up and turned to me. "We need to eat. Let's go." Typical Doaks: food first, police work second. We left my office and headed to Rosa's. Why? Today was meatloaf day, and Doaks never misses meatloaf day at Rosa's.

We were just about to leave Rosa's when O'Neill and Clutch appeared at our table. "Leaving so soon?" O'Neill laughed.

"Yes, we have more police work to do," I responded.

"OK, just wait one minute. Clutch has to talk to Doaks, and I need to talk to you," O'Neill said. I got up, left the table, and headed toward my car.

O'Neill walked beside me and whispered, "Are we still on for dinner tonight?"

I thought about it for a few seconds, then turned and told him, "Yes." O'Neill then asked if it was OK for him to pick me up at my house around 7:00 p.m. I nodded, then left to start the car.

Doaks came out five minutes later, shaking his head and swearing. "That d —n Clutch, wants me to go over to this address on Point Colony and cold knock on the door at this residence," he blurted out.

"What is the address?" I asked. Doaks read it off. "That address is two houses north of Salsa's home!" I said.

Doaks looked at me and said, "OK! Let's go!"

We arrived at the address Clutch gave him. We knocked on the door and waited. After a minute, Doaks pounded on the door, and we waited again. Clutch had told Doaks to ask for a woman named Valencia Gomez. A few seconds later, there was movement in the house, and we saw a reflection of a person from a hallway mirror. Doaks moved to one side of the door; I was on the other. We both had our hands on our guns, just in case.

The door creaked open about an inch. A female voice asked, "Who are you?"

Doaks took out his badge case, put it into his left hand, and told the woman, "Hi, my name is Sgt. Doaks of the Mangrove County Sheriff's Department. Can I talk to you for a second?" The door creaked open another inch, but the chain latch was still hooked. The woman asked to see Doaks' identification again. This time he put his badge and ID right at the woman's eye level.

She said, "Thank you. Please come in." Doaks and I cautiously entered the front hallway. The woman, dressed in a cover up, immediately asked if we wanted coffee, tea, or water.

Doaks looked at her and said, "Nothing for me." I said the same. The woman then turned and asked us to join her in the living room. We followed her and sat down. "Ma'am?" Doaks asked, "can we ask you a few questions?"

"Sure, how can I help you both?" she responded.

Doaks continued, "First can we know your name?"

"Sure, my name is Valencia Gomez. If you can wait, I'll see if I can find my Georgia driver's license," she said. She immediately got up, returned in ten seconds, and handed Doaks her Georgia driver's license.

He continued, "Thank you, Ms. Gomez. We need to ask you a few more questions, ok?"

"Sure, please, ask away. I don't get much company, let alone a great looking male police detective, so please feel free," she said. Doaks was blushing. I turned away to stop my laugh. Doaks then totally lost his train of thought, so I jumped in.

"Ms. Gomez, how long have you been living here?"

"I moved into this VRBO about two weeks ago. I have it rented for six months, but I am not sure how long I will stay here," she said.

"Thanks. During that time, have you visited any of the local restaurants in Point Colony, like the Hut?" I asked.

"No, I haven't gotten out too much lately. I am recovering from a major operation. My mobility is still limited, but, once I am better, I expect to visit all of the restaurants in the local area and the rest of the Keys," she said.

I then asked her one more question. "Do you have any family or friends living in Key Marathon?"

"No," she shared. "I lost my husband last year to cancer, and then I had my hip replaced last month—so I am still trying to work through all of this here."

Doaks regained his composure and asked Ms. Gomez one more question. "Have you travelled outside of the United States in the past four to six months?"

"No, but I have a passport. We were planning a trip to Cambodia in July, but my husband's unexpected death occurred, and I cancelled the trip," she muttered in a sad voice.

Doaks then rose, telling her, "Please, don't get up. We appreciate the time you spent with us, and here is my card. I put my private cell number on the card in case you needed any police assistance while you are visiting here." Ms. Gomez smiled, and I thought I saw her wink at Doaks, but I wasn't sure. I noticed that Doaks was now racing out of the living room and heading directly out of the house. I too thanked Ms. Gomez and left.

Once in the car, I looked at Doaks and asked, "Why are you blushing? And why did you leave in such a hurry?"

"Shut up, Rookie! I don't want to talk about it with you or anyone, so please keep your mouth shut and drive me back to HQ!"

I said, "Yes, sir!" and saluted.

Doaks looked at me and flipped me off. "Get me to HQ now!" he ordered, and off we went.

Ten minutes later we pulled into the sheriff's department. Doaks took off, and I went to check out Valencia Gomez's identification. I ran her Georgia driver's license and found that she appeared to be legit. Something was bugging me about her, though, so I did some digging. I also sent a text to Clutch, asking him to join me in my office. Clutch appeared in one minute.

"What's up, Hood?"

"Listen, we checked out Valencia Gomez. She appears to be legit, but I have a nagging feeling she is not. Can you run her driver's license number in some other data banks, just to make me feel better?"

Clutch looked at me and shook his head. "What is with you, Hood? You can do this just as fast as I can. Why am I doing this?"

"Listen, Clutch, I have a feeling—and when I've had this feeling in the past, it generally tells me to recheck what I just checked. So do me a *big* favor, please, and run Gomez through your connections, and remember—we didn't recognize Maria when she went to the airport, Doaks did. Just run her, and thanks," I said. Clutch grabbed my printouts and left the room a little pissed off, but I didn't care. I felt there was something about Ms. Valencia Gomez, and I wanted all bases covered.

O'Neill popped into my office. "Hood, what did you do to get Clutch all worked up?"

"Well, Doaks and I visited a possible address of a potential individual who may or may not be connected to Maria's return to Key Marathon. We met with a Valencia Gomez, who was a middle-aged woman, in her fifties, with lots of gray hair and wrinkles. Clutch asked Doaks to check her out. I went with him to help and found this woman living at the address Clutch gave us," I stated.

"Interesting," O'Neill said. "I have heard—or seen—the name of Valencia Gomez somewhere; I just can't remember where. Did you run it through the new database?"

"Crud, no, I didn't. Let me do that now while you're here," I said. I ran the name through the new database and found three pages of printed materials on a female in her mid-fifties with the name Valencia Gomez. I printed all of the information from my computer, then placed it on my desk. "I am going to get myself some coffee. Do you want anything?"

O'Neill looked at me. Then, with a twinkle in his eye, he said, "Yes. I would like you to dress up for tonight's dinner date, ok?"

"OK," I said. "See you at my house around 7:00 p.m.," I told him as I left for coffee.

Chapter Twenty-One:
Date Night

October 15, 2021

I got home a little early that day. I told Doaks that I was leaving to take a nap and then work up my findings on Valencia Gomez. I arrived home around 5:00 p.m. *What the heck am I going to wear tonight?* I thought to myself as I was looking through my closet. O'Neill had said to "wear something nice tonight." *What the heck is something nice?*

After getting a little glass of red wine, I selected a white cotton dress. I got myself ready and waited about five minutes on the sofa until the doorbell rang. O'Neill arrived in a sports coat, nice dress shirt, slacks, and shoes that were highly spit shined.

I let him in and asked, "Would you like a glass of wine or something?"

O'Neill replied, "No, thank you, but maybe later." He then said, "We have to go because I have something special planned for this evening."

We got into a non-departmental car. "Where did you get this car?" I asked.

"This is my own private car. I love these new Corvettes, and I had one of mine driven down here last week. I don't like the federal-issued vehicles—and I like the color white. All federal vehicles are either gray or black. I like my white car, and I like that it goes fast!" With that, we left my house in a cloud of smoke. *Interesting way to leave*, I thought but kept my mouth shut.

We arrived at the Isla Bella Beach Resort and Spa around 7:30 p.m. We drove up a small driveway and into a one-car parking space adjacent to a bungalow. O'Neill got out and opened my door, and I got out. We walked into a secluded entryway and were seated by a waiter dressed in a tuxedo. Within seconds, a chef and an assistant chef appeared at our table, asking if we would like a drink. I ordered some Moscato and O'Neill ordered a Crown and Coke. I looked around and tried not to gasp because the place was gorgeous. I have lived in Key Marathon for seven years, and I did not know a place like this existed. I was still gawking when our drinks arrived. O'Neill proposed a toast—I was getting uncomfortable, but I smiled. He toasted to us, closing the hunt on Maria, and looking to what the future holds. I clinked my glass and took a swallow. *Whoa*, I thought to myself, *that is some fantastic wine!* I don't think I had ever had a Moscato tasting that good. I was about to say something when the assistant chef appeared with an elegant menu. I opened the first page and saw exactly what I wanted: a lobster dinner. O'Neill took about the same amount of time when we both looked at each other and said, "I am ready to order!" We laughed.

I placed my order; O'Neill followed. "OK," I said, "do you want me to go first, or do you want to go first?"

O'Neill laughed again. "You can go first."

For the next thirty minutes or so, I went over my career in law enforcement, my goals in life, and my feelings on relationships. O'Neill smiled a lot during my speech, and he didn't interrupt me once. Once I was finished, I nodded, and he started talking about his life. Over the next thirty minutes, I learned a lot about this man. He told me that he was a Navy Seal who retired, joined the FBI, and became a special agent in charge of an elite government team licensed to do a lot of the dirty work no one hears about on television. He had done this type of work over the past decade. He then explained that he would like to retire in five years and do consulting work for anyone or any company that wanted to hire him. Our dinners came while he was talking. We paused, then I told him to please continue. This was the first time I had ever felt comfortable in giving my "date" some background on my life. O'Neill said about the same thing as I was finishing my lobster.

"Interesting" I said, "we both feel comfortable discussing our personal lives. By the way," I whispered to him, "this is the best lobster I have ever—and I mean *ever*—had in the Keys!"

"Thank you for the compliment," O'Neill said. "I wanted

to impress you for a reason." Then he asked me the million-dollar question: "How do you feel about dating?" I was sort of expecting that.

I took another sip of my Moscato, then said, "I have to meet the right person. It has to feel right."

"Thanks," O'Neill said, "I appreciate knowing your thoughts on that, and thank you!" *Crud*, I thought to myself, *did I just ruin this wonderful evening?*

O'Neill then put his glass down and said, "Katie, I would like to start dating you if you are OK with it. Like you, I have had some relationships—not anything serious, but I have always felt if I could meet the right person, I would date again. And I would like to date you."

Interesting conversation again, I thought. I took a few seconds to look out at the ocean, then to look at this wonderful bungalow. Then I looked him straight in the eyes and said, "Yes!" Once we had overcome that hurdle, the rest of the evening was a blast. We talked about interesting cases we both had worked. We shared some upcoming developments in the fields of forensics, data mining, and crime scene investigation. We talked for hours it seemed—but after dessert, coffee, and a short walk on the beach, we looked at our watches and decided it was time to go home.

We were heading back to my place when O'Neill drove slowly down my street. He told me to look straight ahead and not to look on my right. He said, "I need you to let me come into your house right after I park the car. Then I want you to call 911 and get your deputies rolling here ASAP!"

"Are you talking about the guy who ducked down in his vehicle about three cars back?" I asked.

"No, he was five cars back," O'Neill muttered. We arrived at my house. O'Neill got out, then opened my door and I got out. We entered my house. Within seconds, O'Neill was out my back door drawing a bead on this photographer person or whomever he was. I dialed 911 and got my department responding. Then I put on my running shoes, pulled on a pair of shorts under my dress, and went out the back door and crept along my fence. I saw O'Neill sneak up along the driver's side of the car and, within nanoseconds, this guy was airborne, out of his seat, and on the ground. I was ready to cuff him, but O'Neill had done that already and was yanking the guy off the ground, escorting him to the rear of his car. I turned on my phone light and found several items on the front seat. There was a large envelope of photographs—pictures of O'Neill and me. There were several photographs of O'Neill leaving the sheriff's department during the past week, during all times of the day and night. Interestingly, there was a picture of O'Neill, with something written in Arabic (or similar language), stating something about killing him (O'Neill) and a ten-million-dollar reward. I was going to photograph all of this when two of my deputies came roaring onto my street running Code 3—light and sirens. I identified myself to the deputies and had them take over the crime scene processing in the photographer's car.

In the meantime, O'Neill had taken the individual and placed him in the rear seat of one of the deputies' vehicles. He then asked me to follow him back to HQ, where he and I could talk to this person. The deputies processing the car called a tow truck to have the vehicle towed to our garage for additional processing. One of the deputies motioned for me to come over. I did, and he showed me a unique TEC- 9 equipped with a silencer, extended magazine, and armor penetrating bullets.

"Dang," I said. I told the deputy to wait there while I called O'Neill over to look at this find. I stayed with the suspect while O'Neill went over to the deputy. O'Neill put on some gloves, looked at the weapon, and knew instantly who made that model of gun and where these bullets were manufactured.

Shaking his head, he muttered, "Those Al Qaeda b - -s must still be pissed off after Osama Bin Laden (OBL) was hit! Dang, I didn't know my bounty was that high! I guess I have to change my lifestyle now!" He came back to the patrol car chuckling to himself.

I looked at him with an inquisitive quirk on my face. "What gives?"

O'Neill shook his head and said, "Hood, I think Al Qaeda is still pissed off since we assisted our boys in taking out Bin Laden. Now they've put contracts on all the members of my elite squad. These guys are serious—did you see those green tips on those bullets? The green tips mean armor piercing; the red tips are incendiary. I guess I need to make another call to alert my squad that trouble is here and coming for all of us."

"Great, what does all this mean?" I asked.

O'Neill shook his head and threw me his car keys. "Can you please drive my car over to HQ, where we can interrogate this person? Plan on taking tomorrow morning off. I expect he won't be talking to us right away."

O'Neill left in the patrol car. I told the officers to complete their scene processing and then follow the tow company with the car to the sheriff's garage for additional processing. I went back home, changed clothes, and left. I was looking forward to driving O'Neill's Corvette. I love fast cars, but I generally only look at them. Now I was able to actually drive one, so I too spun the tires leaving home and fishtailed at the stop sign at the top of my road. I was having fun!

By 3:00 a.m. on October 16, O'Neill had learned that our photographer's name was Ali Hussain. He was a student at the University of Miami studying computer science and had at least three aliases. O'Neill was paging Johnson to come in once we had this information to verify that the individual was actually Ali Hussain and not someone else. O'Neill said that he recognized his name from several operations in the Middle East over the past ten years and had already contacted his partners to get a team into Miami to search Hussain's apartment. The deputies processing the scene at my house came into the interrogation room to talk to me.

"Detective Hood, we think you need to come with us to look at something we found in this guy's trunk." I told O'Neill

I would be back and followed them into the garage. There I saw that the truck lid was open, and I looked in. Inside the trunk was what looked like a drone. There was also a cylinder device, with some government numbers stenciled on the tube, and I knew it was time to call Clutch.

He arrived at 4:00 a.m., scratching his head and looking like he had just rolled out of bed. "Hood, what the h – -l?"

"Clutch," I said, "I got you up so you can see the interesting surprise we found in the trunk of this guy's car."

"OK," he said, "let's see this surprise." He took a look. "Holy s - - t, this is serious stuff here! Did you search for anything else?" The deputies shook their heads. They had found these and gotten me here ASAP. I took the cue from Clutch's look and began to carefully search the trunk, taking everything out very carefully. Under the spare tire—which wasn't a spare tire but an imitation spare tire—I found two black boxes, each about thirteen inches long and four inches wide. I processed them, then had Clutch come over to look at the boxes. On them were some more government stenciling and some other numbers I did not recognize.

"Clutch," I said, "can you tell me anything about these boxes or these tubes?"

"No, but let me make two calls and within an hour I will have someone here who knows all about these two things!"

At 4:30 a.m. dispatch notified Clutch and O'Neill that their visitor from the government was waiting in the lobby. Clutch sent me, and I went out to our lobby. There stood Ret.

Sgt. Major Steven Bourne.

"Hello again," he said.

I laughed and held out my hand. "Ret. Sgt. Major Bourne, why am I not surprised?"

"Well, I just happened to be in the area, and thought I would stop by and see what kind of interesting tubes and boxes you have just found," he replied. Off we went—Bourne knew exactly where to go. As we entered the processing garage, Clutch, O'Neill, and now Johnson all greeted him.

"So, we need your expertise again, although I didn't know you were an expert in unmanned aerial vehicles (UAVs)," Clutch said.

Bourne shook his head and said, "You would be surprised what this old goat knows." He then looked at the case and the two small boxes. He took out his phone, photographed both items, and sent the pictures off (who knows where). Seconds later, he got an answer. "These items were stolen off a boat shipment last month to Ukraine. Both have been reported stolen, and there are at least another dozen similar tubes and black boxes still missing from the same shipment."

Clutch looked at Bourne. "So, in English, what are these things and how do they work?"

Bourne asked us, "Have you done any type of bomb search on this vehicle since you brough it here?"

"No, crap," Clutch replied. Bourne suggested that we all back away from the vehicle, take the two items found in the trunk, secure them in the property/evidence weapons locker, and leave the area.

Five minutes later, Sgt. Mutt appeared with his K-9 unit and searched the vehicle. Within a minute, the dog alerted on the right front fender. The bomb techs appeared a few minutes later and found a bomb strapped to the fender well with a green light blinking. Bourne then asked O'Neill whether he'd found any car keys on the suspect in custody.

"Yes, I confiscated these keys seconds after I cuffed that S.O.B."

"Good," Bourne said. "Can I see his keys?"

O'Neill went back to the property and evidence locker, opened one, and took out the car's ignition keys. He returned and gave them to Bourne.

"Thanks. Now if I could ask someone to get me a knife, I will defuse this weapon," Bourne said. *Crud, crud, and crud, who is this guy?* I wondered again. *He knows way too much about some serious things.* Seconds later, Bourne had defused the car's keys. He proceeded to show all of us the arming mechanism built into the key fob and asked O'Neill, "Have you searched your suspect completely?"

"Yes," O'Neill winced, "but I can search him again."

"Please do. Can you take off his shoes? And has he been cuffed with both hands since you arrested him?" Bourne asked.

Crap, O'Neill and I thought to ourselves. "He has had both hands cuffed to the bar on the table in our interrogation room," O'Neill groaned.

"Good. If you don't mind, please get the suspect's shoes,

and bring them to me," Bourne whispered. O'Neill came back seconds later with a pair of leather loafers. "Thanks," Bourne replied as he took the loafers. Within seconds, Bourne had ripped off both heels, and there inside the right heel was yet another small device. "Here, you all can see one of the smallest personal bombs ever made. OBL was developing them before we got him, and, given this evidence now, I believe our Al Qaeda friends have mastered putting them into service."

Does it ever end, I thought to myself. *Jeez, these guys have drones, miniature bombs in the heels of a shoe, and God know what is in the black box we took out of the spare tire well.* Just as I was about to speak up, dispatch came on the intercom, requesting that Clutch or O'Neill come to the lobby for the four men in Navy uniforms asking for Ret. Sgt. Major Bourne.

"Hood!" Clutch bellowed.

"Yes!"

"Please check with Bourne to see if he called in some Navy support!" *Dang, I guess I am the errand girl today.*

But Bourne came over to me and whispered, "You just stay put; I will get my demolition team here in a second." He then ambled off down the hallway into the lobby.

At 5:30 a.m. the sheriff, the undersheriff, and Mr. Moceri were present in the conference room. Everyone looked fresh, showered, and full of energy. I, on the other hand, was still wrapping my head around what had happened in the past six hours. Clutch made more introductions; then Mr. Moceri asked about the status of the suspect.

Bourne spoke up and told everyone that the two items found in the suspect's car were stolen federal property. O'Neill added that the suspect had in his control a TEC-9 with a silencer and green tip bullets. Both the silencer and green tip bullets were illegal to possess, according to federal law.

Mr. Moceri asked, "So the suspect in our custody will be charged with several federal offenses, correct?"

O'Neill and Bourne both answered, "Yes." O'Neill looked at Johnson, who added more information.

"Actually, the suspect Ali Hussain is wanted on several international charges for the assassination of two Israeli town leaders and one Israeli general." *Oh, great,* I said to myself, *now we have drones, bombs, and assassins in the Keys. What's next?* I was just about to ask a question when Bourne asked the four Navy officers to bring in the objects found in the suspect's trunk. In the middle of the conference room, the objects were laid on the table. Bourne and another Navy officer with a lot of ribbons on his chest slowly opened the cylinder-shaped device and pulled out an object. Within seconds, the object was unfolded, and a drone resembling a switchblade appeared.

The Navy officer said, "This is an AeroVironment Switchblade drone. This drone is a Model 600 and can blow up tanks. It can be launched from any location, has a range of ten kilometers, and can fly for twenty-five minutes."

Then Bourne asked the Navy officer to open the black box. "Here is the updated nano drone version called the *Black Hornet,*

Bourne explained. "This is a nano drone made by Prox Dynamics AS of Norway. This drone, as you can see, is about four inches long and one inch wide. It has a range of one mile with a flying time of twenty to twenty-five minutes. The drone has been modified to include an explosive warhead embedded in the nose camera and can kill up to three people, depending on where the drone is directed. These two drones are in a two pack in this box; they can come in a one, two, or six pack."

"Dang," O'Neill chuckled. "Like beer," he whispered in my ear. Bourne shot a look at O'Neill and continued his drone discussion.

"These drones we just captured have been modified. Both are capable of killing a number of people and can stop cars or other vehicles." He continued, "I believe we now need to reconsider our next steps carefully. Your suspect Maria Hernandez may or may not have access to these drones. If she does, then, sheriff, you need to advise your officers of a new lethal threat facing them as your task force closes in on her location. O'Neill, you know what to do given this latest find?"

"Yes," O'Neill said, then left the room. I looked at the ceiling in our room and thought, *Good Lord, what else can happen tonight?* Twenty minutes later I was ordered to go home, get some rest, and report back to HQ after noon.

Chapter Twenty-Two:
The Dome and The Fight

October 16, 2021

It was 11:30 a.m. when I woke up, turned off my alarm clock, and got my coffee. The interrogation of Hussain, the debriefing on the drones, and all of the pending changes coming to our area gave me a monster headache. I had gotten home at 5:45 a.m., slept for a while, then got up to face another outstanding day.

I was heading out the door when Doaks called and started barking orders at me. He ranted for five minutes until I told him, "Shut up and listen to me." When he did, I told him about my last twelve hours, the arrest and search of the assassin's car, the drones, and the new equipment coming.

Doaks barked, "Why didn't you call me? I would have been there in a heartbeat!"

"Yeah, I know that, but with this assassin suspect, then the feds getting involved, that Bourne guy showing up with more military people, and then the sheriff appearing, it was way outside my comfort zone. I decided to inform you today when you got to work. Oh, how did you sleep last night?" I asked him.

"Hood, one of these days," his voice trailed off and then I heard in the background the sheriff asking him to get me back to HQ ASAP.

I told Doaks, "I heard all of that. I'll be there in fifteen minutes or less." Leaving my house and jumping into my patrol vehicle, I was now wondering, *Why the heck does the sheriff want me now?*

I arrived at Headquarters to find a number of military vehicles and equipment in our secure parking lot. I entered HQ and went to my desk. I had almost made it to my office when Doaks, O'Neill, and Clutch saw me. They all approached.

I was about to run when O'Neill said, "Please, come with us—we need to update you and Doaks on the latest intel." We trundled into the conference room. There in the middle of a lot of activity was Ret. Sgt. Major Bourne. *Surprise, surprise*, I thought to myself. *Who is this guy?* O'Neill told us to take a seat; a major teleconference was about to begin. He told Doaks and me, "Do *not* say one word during this conference—just listen very carefully because your lives will depend on it!" When the teleconference began, there were fifteen people on the television screen. All of them were federal or state officials with various titles: the governor of Florida, the director of DPS, and two federal prosecutors, among others. The director of the FBI introduced a person in charge of DARPA (Defense Advanced Research Projects Agency), a super intelligence agency.

For the next ten minutes, this person told us we would be implementing some new technology involving a drone detection/protection system. In addition, several other new technologies would be located in our sheriff's protected area. These devices included drone killers, drone monitoring equipment, and a new device called *HPM* (a high-powered microwave device) that generated EMPs (electromagnetic pulses) to destroy drones.

I was lost after the first three minutes of this conversation. Too many letters, too much technology, and my head was pounding.

Doaks looked at me and whispered in my ear, "Hood, this is Star Wars stuff!" I nodded, then reached inside my pocket for Ibuprofen. The conference dragged on for another twenty minutes. I was too lost and confused to understand most if not all of the terms, initials, and federal talk. Once the conference was done, Clutch came over and looked at me and Doaks.

"Hood, you look like you tied one on, and Doaks, you are looking just lovely—*not*." Doaks was about to flip him off, but I stopped him.

"Clutch, can we go get some coffee, and can you please translate all of this garble we just heard?" I pleaded.

"Sure, let's get some fresh coffee, perhaps a doughnut or a raisin bar—or something courtesy of the feds—and go to your office," he suggested, exiting the conference room. Doaks took two doughnuts, claiming he hadn't had breakfast. I grabbed an apple, and Clutch had three coffees in his hands. In my office, Clutch sat down, then looked at me and Doaks.

"Well, we are now privileged to have the latest technology in drones: drone technology, drone detection, and drone destruction located here for the next month or so."

"What the h - -l," Doaks squawked. "Why do we need all of this?"

Clutch was about to answer when I interrupted. "Doaks, last night or this morning, we arrested this assassin. We found several drones in various sizes inside his trunk and lots of intel indicating that Al Qaeda had put a ten-million-dollar contract on O'Neill and his elite squad. Bourne showed up, and then all of this equipment and conference occurred."

Doaks looked at me and Clutch. "So what the h - - l is going on?"

For the next fifteen minutes, Clutch briefed Doaks and me on what was happening now and why it was happening. Clutch stated that the drones we found in the assassin's car were unique; in fact, Bourne was upset at his contacts because they did *not* have any intel that any terrorist group had redesigned these drones to become killer drones. Clutch continued, "Bourne had gone into hyper speed putting together the teleconference call and getting this unique equipment here. This equipment represents some of the latest technology in drone defense. The Iron Curtain Dome we discussed in our teleconference is an active protective system used to prevent drones from coming into specific areas. This system is backed up by another drone monitoring system with four key elements: detection, radio frequency analyzers, acoustic sensors, and drone detection radar called *Elvira*. In addition, the feds have integrated a high-powered microwave device that can generate electromagnetic pulses (EMPs) that destroy drones. One other item is now at our disposal—drone killers, which are drones that can seek and destroy other drones, including some nano drones we found in the assassin's trunk."

Doaks looked at me and crossed his eyes. I hit him and said "Stop!" Clutch saw part of this, and we all had a laugh. "Jeez," I said, "Star Wars in Key Marathon. This is totally nuts!"

The rest of the day was spent learning how to deal with all of this new technology. O'Neill grabbed my arm and directed me into an open office. "Hey," he said, "I wanted to thank you for last night. I really enjoyed being with you." Then he kissed me.

"Whoa," I said after lingering just long enough for him to finish his kiss. "I really enjoyed last night, too, and thank you for giving me one of the best date nights I have been on in a long time!" He then asked me how I was doing with a few hours of sleep and now all of this new technology. I told him I was still sleepy, but I was learning quickly how to use this new technology.

"Good," he said, "because we are now playing a new game in the Keys. Drones, and attack drones, are the new battlefield in this game, and I do *not* want anyone, particularly you, getting killed by one of these things."

"I got it," I said. "And by the way, I don't want you to get killed either. It seems you are the main target. The rest of us are just collateral damage," I mentioned as I pulled him close to me and kissed him. That little interlude lasted another minute but was interrupted because I was getting paged by dispatch. When O'Neill let me go, I waved and left the area.

I called dispatch on my phone. The operator had a person on hold asking for me. I told her to put the call through. "Hello, this is Detective Hood, how can I help you?"

"Detective Hood, this is Valencia Gomez. I was wondering if you and that other man—what is his name, Doaks?—could come over in ten minutes?"

"Sure, can I tell Sgt. Doaks what this is about?"

"I can tell you I think I have some information on a woman named Maria something. Can you guys be here in ten minutes?" Gomez asked.

"Sure, we'll be there." I hung up. *Strange*, I thought, *why is she calling me and not Doaks?* My sixth sense kicked in. *Something is not right here*, I thought. I switched on my computer to run the name of Valencia Gomez again through our new database. Two minutes later, the screen lit up. "Holy crap!" I yelled. Valencia Gomez was one of the aliases Maria Hernandez has used in the past. I queried the database for any kind of pictures on this name.

I called Doaks, Clutch, and O'Neill all at the same time.

Clutch and O'Neill were back in my office in minutes. Doaks, well, he ambled into my office five minutes after everyone else. I was briefing Clutch and O'Neill on the possibility that Doaks and I were walking into an ambush when Doaks arrived. He looked at all of us, then sat down. "Am I late?"

Clutch was just about to open his mouth when I jumped in and said, "Doaks, where the heck were you? We got a major lead in finding Maria! Where were you?"

Doaks dropped his gaze, then said, "I was in the men's room."

"Great, now sit in the chair, and listen, but *don't* say a word," I ordered. The next fifteen minutes consisted of planning and chaos. O'Neill then Clutch, then Clutch then O'Neill were putting together plans on how Doaks and I were to approach the address of Valencia Gomez. Finally, after fifteen minutes of frantic planning, Clutch threw up the peace sign, and he and O'Neill agreed on the plan. Doaks and I would go to Gomez's address. We would not approach the door until two drones were up around her house and one nano drone had flown into her yard to look inside the house. Our SWAT team was going to be in place adjacent to the fenced walls along the house. Then Doaks and I would approach the front door. Prior to knocking on the door, I would put a micro camera underneath the door to check for any IEDs attached to the door or to anything in the area. If the drones and the micro camera indicated that the door appeared to be safe, Doaks would knock on the door, and we both would wait outside the entrance, hugging the entry walls.

Doaks and I suited up with our ballistics vests and tactical gear. Clutch and O'Neill had two drones and a nano drone up and ready at the Gomez location within five minutes. The SWAT team was en route to our suspect's address. Doaks was in the men's room for the next five minutes. I was praying to the good Lord that no one would be hurt in what we all were about to do. Doaks came to my office and said, "You're driving; let's go."

We headed to the Gomez location. We got there in fifteen minutes, a lot later than the ten minutes when Gomez had wanted us to arrive. The SWAT team was in place, the drones had viewed the location, and the nano drone had been able to see inside the house, in the kitchen area, and in the door entry area. The place looked deserted, and there appeared to be no IEDs. After checking with the SWAT commander, Clutch, and O'Neill, we exited my vehicle and slowly approached the front door. I had the micro camera cable feed under the door in seconds and looked at the view camera. It indicated that nothing appeared to be attached to the door or door handle, nor was any trip wire located in the entryway. Clutch and O'Neill saw the screen too and gave us the go-ahead to knock on the door. We knocked, waited, then we knocked again—but again, nothing. Then Doaks grabbed the door handle and pushed.

The door flew open, and a series of automatic weapons began firing from inside the windows and inside the door.

Doaks and I dove behind the entry walls, and the SWAT team initiated their countermeasures. Within five minutes, SWAT team members had located and disarmed the automatic weapons, which had been placed in several locations. Just as the SWAT team was coming to my car, the on-site SWAT commander ordered everyone out immediately. Seconds later the entire house exploded.

Immediately the SWAT commander was trying to ascertain the condition of all his team members. Luckily, no one was seriously injured. It was then that Doaks got a phone call on his private cellphone. The caller ID indicated that a V. Gomez was on the phone. Doaks answered the call and heard, "You're still alive. Too bad. I look forward to seeing you die soon, Doaks." Then the caller hung up.

Doaks looked at me and was about to speak when suddenly the SWAT vehicle parked at the end of the street exploded. O'Neill directed all of us to immediately leave the area on foot. He yelled, "Get out now!" We started running from the scene when another police vehicle blew up. Doaks looked at me and yelled, "What the h - -l is going on?" I was just about to answer him when I heard a high-pitched whine; then above us in the sky, there was another explosion.

"Drones and drone killers," I told him. We left the area and headed down the road to the main highway. Life in Key Marathon had just changed, and I could only imagine what was going to happen next.

Chapter Twenty-Three:

Death and Destruction

October 16, 2021: Later that day

Doaks and I got back to the department about an hour later. As we arrived in our parking area, our department looked like a military base preparing for an attack. There were several military trucks with microwave dishes, some type of rifle-looking weapons on some other trucks, and a number of tube-looking devices set up around the fenced area. Doaks looked at me and said, "Star Wars in Key Marathon. I would have never guessed it would come to this."

I was heading to get my second cup of coffee when O'Neill and Bourne showed up at my office door. "Hood, can you please come with us? We need to debrief you on what happened at the Gomez house," O'Neill ordered.

"Sure, can I bring my coffee and perhaps grab an apple along the way?" I asked.

"Yes," O'Neill agreed; then we left and entered a small, secluded office outside the conference room.

"What is going on?" I asked.

Before O'Neill could answer, Bourne jumped into the conversation. "Listen, I want you to tell me in your own words what happened after the house exploded."

I took a sip of coffee, then looked at both of them. "I don't remember too much. The explosion was loud, and my ears were ringing for at least two to three minutes afterward. I do remember someone ordering me and Doaks to leave the area, not to use our cars, and get out. I am not sure I can recall anything after that," I said.

"OK," Bourne continued, "how long after the house exploded before the SWAT vehicle blew up?"

I looked up to the ceiling, thought a little more, took a bite of my apple, and said, "I don't know."

"Can you think about the question again? I am trying to determine if it was about a minute or two or less than a minute."

"Why is that important?" I asked.

"Because we believe that the drone that hit the SWAT vehicle was a switchblade model and that the drone that hit the patrol vehicle was the same type of drone," Bourne replied.

I was racking my aching brain when Doaks poked his head into the small room and blurted out, "I think the first drone hit about 50 seconds after the house exploded."

How did he know that was the question I was asked? I wondered.

"If we can figure out the timing of these two drone hits,

we can triangulate a possible location for the home base," Doaks replied.

O'Neill, then Bourne, looked in awe at Doaks. "You are exactly right," Bourne said. "How did you figure that out? Good detective work!" he said and left the area. Again, I thought, *Doaks sometimes just amazes me!*

O'Neill looked at me and shook his head. "Sometimes Doaks comes up with stuff that is scary. He was absolutely right on the triangulation. Given his answer, we may be able to locate the home base in a few minutes," Bourne said before leaving.

O'Neill looked at me and asked, "Are you injured in any way?"

"No, I just wish I had acted sooner on the Gomez woman. She played both of us with her disguises and her attitude."

"Next time, we'll get her. Just wait," O'Neill sighed. Then he left me alone in the office.

Clutch came looking for me about an hour after my debriefing session. He was concerned about something, so he asked me to come with him to a room off of the conference room. We arrived, and he asked, "Are you all right?"

"Yes, I'm fine. My ears are still ringing, but my headache is gone," I replied.

His face immediately showed signs of relief. "Let's talk about what may be coming." For the next hour, Clutch brainstormed with me on what loose ends we were missing in our case. These areas were identified: Maria was back, and we needed to find her; the drone base needed to be located and destroyed; the Tongs would retaliate, so we needed to be prepared for another attack. These three areas needed to be put up on our whiteboard in front of our task force, and we needed to throw all of our intel into solving these three issues. Clutch then left and headed back to the conference room.

I went to the ladies' room and took an inventory. I looked like crap. Everything on me—my face, eyes, hair, clothing, everything—looked like I had been in a bar fight and lost. *Hood, you look awful! Why don't you go home, rest, and come back,* I said to myself. I thought I was alone, but the sheriff's new secretary came out of a stall, looked at me, and nodded her head.

"Detective Hood, you need to go home, rest, and come back later. The department can get along without you for an hour or so." I looked in the mirror again and left.

I was heading out the door when Doaks and O'Neill came over to my office door. "Going somewhere, Hood?" Doaks asked.

"Yes. I am going home. I need about a two-hour nap, a shower, and to change my clothes," I replied to both of them.

"Whoa, there, my friend! You need to have someone go with you!" O'Neill ordered.

"Why?" I retorted.

"I am very concerned that your house may now be under some type of surveillance, and once you are inside, I anticipate that a drone attack could occur or that an IED has already been planted inside. You cannot go home without a bomb dog and an escort making sure your house is clear and that you are safe inside your home and free from drone attacks," O'Neill said.

"OK, who is getting the bomb dog ready to search my house, and who is going to be the expert in preventing drones from attacking my home?" I asked.

Doaks looked at O'Neill, then at me. "Rookie, I will get the dog and the bomb guys headed your way."

Great, I thought, *one out of two isn't bad*. I then looked at O'Neill.

He said, "I will go with you. I have some pull on getting this new surveillance system operational, and I may be able to put up a drone shield for the next hour or so."

Crud, I thought, *O'Neill in my home, while I am sleeping? No!* But I nodded my head and said, "Thanks."

Twenty minutes later, the bomb squad and the dog had begun to search my home. The search found not one but two IEDs planted in my bathroom and in my door entry. Both of the IEDs were dismantled. O'Neill then made a few calls, and supposedly the new drone protection shields were up. He came into my kitchen, put his arms around me, and asked, "Do you need help in the shower or in any other area?" I half-heartedly pushed him away and told him to make himself at home and that I would be down in twenty minutes or so. O'Neill looked dejected as he turned and left my kitchen. I told him the coffee maker was near the refrigerator, and the coffee and filters were next to the hall cabinet.

Upstairs I was enjoying my long, hot shower. It was wonderful! All of the past twenty-four hours was going down my shower drain. I was just about to get out when O'Neill opened the door, threw a towel at me, grabbed me in his arms, and ran both of us out of the house. He threw me into his car, and we sped away.

"Damn, what the h - -l are you doing?" I shouted at him.

"Sorry, but my watch has a tracking app that just went off. That means there is a drone in the area, and we have about 30 seconds to get out of here." I was just about to say another nasty phrase when we heard the explosion. I turned around, and my house was gone. I was in shock: my house, my stuff, my life had just gone up in smoke and flames. I turned and looked at O'Neill and cried hysterically.

The next twelve hours were a blur. I was taken to a safe house, given some dry clothing, and told to sit down at a table and drink some fresh coffee. I didn't like to be ordered around, but O'Neill had just saved my life—and he had gotten me clothing, coffee, and a safe area. I looked at him and asked him to come over to hold me. He did so and whispered in my ear, "This will work out. Have some patience." *Right*, I thought. *My entire life has been upended. My home, my everything has just been blown up! But I will get past this—God has my back.*

Doaks came flying into my new "home" about 30 minutes after I arrived. He looked at me, then he hugged me. I was in shock. Doaks hugging me?

He let me go and asked, "Rookie, are you OK? What can I do to help; what do you need?" He was nonstop in questions for the next three minutes.

Finally I grabbed him and said, "Hush!" He shook his head and apologized. I gave him a big hug and said, "Ah, I didn't know you cared!"

"Shut up! You are my partner, and partners watch out for each other!" he snorted. I nodded my head in understanding; then I thanked him. It was nice to know I was cared about in my department.

After getting established in the safe house, I had O'Neill bring me back to headquarters to work on finding the drone home base Maria was using to attack us. Bourne was going ballistic. He was furious that a drone (or drones) had been able to get under or through the surveillance dome we had established. He was on the phone to the DARPA people immediately after my house exploded. He wanted no more mistakes. He looked at me when I arrived in the conference room, rushed over, and gave me a hug (after he asked my permission to hug me). He apologized for the failure of our dome of protection and promised me that the federal government would get me another house, clothing, and car once we had completed our job here. Then everyone was back at work, including me.

I went to my desk, pulled up more information on V. Gomez, and began searching for possible locations where she may have chosen to live in Key Marathon.

Chapter Twenty-Four:

More Death and Destruction

October 21, 2021—4:15 a.m.

Flight 9999 was approaching a runway for Key West International Airport. It was 4:15 a.m. when the private jet was on its final approach to Runway 1. Two miles out, the jet descended to its proper altitude and reduced its airspeed. The approach was proceeding as planned when the plane suddenly disappeared from the radar. All of the FAA flight operators immediately focused on the radar screen, while an operator attempted to radio the pilot. The pilot did not respond, and the plane was not on the radar screen. All of the flight operators working in the tower looked to the southeast, the jet's approach direction, but saw nothing but black sky. One operator looked at the administrator and asked, "What happened to this plane?" No one in the tower had any idea why this plane had suddenly dropped off the radar screen with no radio contact. The on-duty administrator initiated the alert notifications that a plane appeared to go down while approaching the airport.

O'Neill, Bourne, and Clutch were notified as part of this alert process. Within minutes all were up and making phone calls. Bourne was not only up, but he had arranged a helicopter to fly him down to the Key West airport. He arrived thirty-five minutes after the plane left the radar. Two military people met him on the runway, and he was immediately driven over to the control tower. Fifty minutes later, one Coast Guard Cutter, two Coast Guard helicopters, and several smaller Coast Guard boats were converging on the last known coordinates of this jet.

Bourne was scouring the flight plans for this flight when the captain of the Cutter radioed him. "Sir, we are at the last known coordinates for this flight, and there is no wreckage in the water. I have ordered my helos to start a grid search over a half-mile radius and my smaller craft to begin a quarter-mile grid search from these last known coordinates. Sir, I am amazed there is no wreckage on site. What suggestions do you have?"

"Are there any boats in the area?" Bourne asked the captain.

"No, sir," he was told.

"OK, please continue your search pattern, and I will re-contact you in sixty minutes." Bourne clicked off the radio. Immediately he was on his phone, typing to his private contacts, R&L. The FAA operators were watching him type when he told them, "I think I know what happened to this jet; I just need to check something out." Three minutes later, a message appeared on his phone. Whatever it said disappeared in one minute. Realizing that the people in the tower were watching him, Bourne said, "Excuse me, I have to go." He left the area.

Clutch and O'Neill were still on their phones when both got an unusual page. This page interrupted their conversations. Both looked at the page, then at each other. "What the heck is this?" Clutch motioned to O'Neill. "I have never, and I mean never, seen this type of message before." Clutch took a screenshot of the message, then suddenly the message had disappeared from his phone. Clutch tried to find it in his deleted files, but there was no indication that a message existed.

"What the heck is this?" O'Neill asked Clutch.

"I don't know. I have never seen a message come on my phone, then disappear, then have no record of a message in any of my phone calls."

Bourne received a call on another cell phone that he pulled out of his pocket. "Hello, Bourne here," he stated. Then he began barking orders to Clutch and O'Neill. First, Bourne told them he had ordered a Navy dive team to go to the coordinates of where this jet plane went down. Next, he asked O'Neill to contact his friends in NSA to get satellite pictures of the area where the jet disappeared. Third, he told O'Neill to contact his space operations group to see if there was an EMP (electromagnetic pulse) burst seen along the Atlantic Ocean near the Key West Airport during the past two hours.

Bourne continued, "I believe this jet was shot down using a THOR (tactical high-power microwave operational responder) device. This device is capable of bringing down a jet aircraft the size and weight of a G800 Gulfstream jet. I believe that the plane went down and sank in the ocean. I also believe that the plane may still be in the water, covered with some type of camouflage to conceal its actual location."

Clutch then mouthed to O'Neill, "Ask Bourne who he thinks could do this."

O'Neill nodded and asked the question.

Bourne hesitated for a minute, then he stated, "I believe Maria Hernandez may have done this. I believe the aircraft shot down belonged to the Tongs gang. I also believe the Tongs had one of their three international bosses on that plane along with a large shipment of automatic weapons. If I am right, we need to alert the secretary of defense and the president on the possible need for additional personnel and specialized equipment sent into our area ASAP!"

O'Neill then asked Bourne what he needed Clutch and him to do.

"Get Johnson's fusion center researching EMPs looking at satellite photos of the Atlantic Ocean over the past three hours, and let me know when the space operations group gets back to you." He hung up.

O'Neill and Clutch looked at each other; then Clutch asked, "How in the world could Maria get this type of weapon?"

The dive team that Maria had hired was completing its tasks. All passengers inside the jet had been killed when the team entered the plane. The plane sank in forty feet of water. The specially designed ocean camouflage had worked perfectly. The leader of the team contacted Maria, saying "Amiga, we are done!"

"Good. Please meet El Jefe at our arranged location, and he will give you your payment," she told him. Thirty minutes later El Jefe met the dive team on a secluded part of Key West. There he gave the team leader $100,000 in cash. He left, and the team disappeared in the darkness.

Bourne, Clutch, and O'Neill were now entering hyperspace speed trying to discover what happened to Flight 9999. Bourne had contacted all of his private sources to determine if a civilian could buy a THOR device on any black market anywhere in the world. Clutch was working with Nguyen trying to find any viable contacts in Thailand, Vietnam, or Cambodia who could provide information on Flight 9999. O'Neill was still collecting pictures and data from the NSA and the space operations group.

I walked into this chaos around 7:00 a.m. I peeked into the conference room, saw the level of activity, and immediately decided I needed some coffee and silence. I left, got coffee, and went into my office. I was working on collecting more data on Maria Hernandez, Valencia Gomez, and any other aliases I could find on this woman. Doaks came in and sat down. He was drinking a cup of coffee and eating another doughnut. "Doaks, you know those things are bad for you," I commented.

"Rookie. This doughnut is a required food group for all cops. It is a further requirement that all rookies should ensure that our conference/coffee area has doughnuts on the table at all times," he chuckled.

"Right, and that will clog your arteries faster than processed cheese," I said.

He made a gesture with his finger, looked at me, and said, "Enough! What are you doing?"

"I am trying to figure out where Maria could be hiding. Can you think of any houses, abandoned buildings, or estates that may have enough space to store the amount of equipment and weapons she might have?"

Doaks looked up to the ceiling—then scratching his head looked down at the floor. "Rookie, I need to look something up. I will get back to you in twenty minutes; then we can go and eat lunch," he said, then left. *Great*, I thought, *more food. At this rate Doaks will have a heart attack sometime in the next year*. Eighteen minutes later, Doaks came into my office with a page of possible locations where buildings/homes/estates had been abandoned or foreclosed. I was amazed.

"Doaks, how did you generate this page of properties?"

"Don't underestimate my skills and investigative techniques," he squawked. I was about to give him an obscene gesture but held back.

"I am amazed at your skills once again," I offered. I was

impressed and took the list from him. "Let's do some recon on each of these locations to see what, if anything, is happening at them." Doaks agreed, so we left my office and headed towards the parking lot.

We entered the highway; then Doaks told me, "Go to Rosa's. Today's lunch special is tacos, and I am starving." Just another day with Sgt. Doaks: food first, police work later.

Maria, Patron, El Jefe, and their army of criminals had anticipated that the police would come looking at abandoned or foreclosed properties on Key Marathon at some point. Maria told Patron to make sure that the guards were well hidden from any outside surveillance and prohibited anyone walking outside during the day. She knew that NSA and several other federal enforcement agencies had access to satellites moving over the skies above her newly established headquarters. The men had done an excellent job in not moving anything or anyone outside the estate during the day. Patron pulled up all of the perimeter video cameras. He scanned all of them around their camera range and shook his head. The men and their equipment were well camouflaged from any prying eyes.

Patron reported to Maria, "The men and their weapons are well hidden from anyone coming into our area. I will ensure that the men stay put during the daylight hours; then we can move the THOR back to our location later this evening."

Maria was down in the basement of this mansion. There in the basement was an assortment of drones, nano drones, several javelin anti-tank weapons, a few MANPATS (man portable antitank weapons), and a few other technologically advanced weapons. Her trip to the Middle East had cost her ninety million dollars in American cash, but she needed the most advanced weapons in the world to take down the Tongs and any others who would challenge her organization. Maria looked skyward and said a short prayer for Salsa: "I will destroy these Tongs and anyone else who helped in killing you, my love! You will be remembered forever!"

Doaks and I had just finished our meals at Rosa's when Doaks looked at me and asked, "Where should we start?"

I said, "We need to find a building or large estate that can house a lot of big equipment and a lot of men. I think we should start at the north part of Key Marathon and work our way south to the 7-mile Bridge."

"Sounds like a plan. Let's go."

Two hours later, we had checked three huge warehouses, one vast estate, and three large garage-type spaces. None of these locations showed any signs of recent or past activity. There were no shoe prints or litter inside and nothing outside each of these areas.

Doaks looked at me and said, "Rookie, one more location;

then we are done."

"OK, off to Coco Plum Drive. What type of building structure do we have here?" I asked.

"This is an old mansion that has gone through fifteen years of construction issues as well as fifteen years of legal wrangling with the Building Planning and Zoning department in the City of Marathon," Doaks quipped.

It was shortly after sunset when we entered an isolated driveway leading to this mansion. Doaks and I were crawling along the driveway in my vehicle when Doaks told me to speed up. I did, and the car traveled about two football fields when a huge mansion appeared in front of us. Doaks was beginning to get out of the car when he took my Kel-Lite and flashed it around. Within two or three seconds, he stuck his head inside and said, "Rookie, we need to get the h - -l out of here now." I nodded my head. He jumped into the car, and we left.

Back on the highway, once we had left the mansion, Doaks turned and said, "Maria is living there! That is her new headquarters."

"How in the world did you come to that conclusion in two or three seconds?" I asked.

"As we were entering the driveway, I noticed three camouflaged cameras on the palm trees, and I saw what appeared to be heavy machine gun nests along the entryway. The last thing I saw was either Patron or El Jefe. One of them was coming around the basement entrance. I think it was Jefe—I know him because he shot and killed one of my best homicide detectives fifteen years ago. I will never forget his face, and today I saw him again at that location."

"Holy crap, you have one set of eagle eyes, Doaks. I missed all of that completely," I said.

Once more, Doaks looked at me and pointed to his head, "Never underestimate my brain." Then he instructed me to head to headquarters while he contacted Clutch and O'Neill. He told them we had discovered Maria's headquarters. It was time to assemble our task force and prepare for a war.

Chapter Twenty-Five:

The Battle

October 26, 2021—11:00 a.m.

Preparations for the battle with Maria's organization were underway. Doaks looked at me as we watched our parking lot become a military war base. "What the heck are those things, and what about these dome-looking devices and these microwave dishes? Dang, it looks like a college football game day with all of these things out here," Doaks quipped.

"Right, but this isn't a college football game—this is our chance to finally, *finally* catch that b - -h and put her away for life!" I grumbled.

"Enough of this," O'Neill muttered, as he had quietly entered my office and told both of us to report to the conference room. The conference room looked like an operations center for the Olympics. There were televisions, computers, and other objects I did not recognize. I was about to say something when Bourne told everyone to grab a seat and listen up.

For the next hour, Bourne gave us the attack plan on Maria's compound. Included in this plan were several things I had never heard of, such as drone killers, zappers, phasers, spoofing equipment, and a few new-looking drones I had never seen. Doaks was looking a little dumbfounded, and I nodded my head in agreement. This was very high-tech stuff, probably a once-in-a-lifetime opportunity to see what technology our government had developed. Bourne stopped for a moment in his presentation to see if anyone had any questions.

Doaks was about to raise his hand when I kicked him under the table. "Don't! I whispered. "Let him finish; then ask." He glared at me but nodded his head in agreement. Bourne then turned the battle attack plan over to some other military guy who at first I did not recognize. Why? Because he was dressed in combat fatigues and wore a strange-looking hat. Then I recognized the person as O'Neill. He was dressed in a military uniform I didn't recognize, and he was all business.

Over the next thirty minutes, he outlined our plan of attack. The attack was planned to start the next day at 2:00 a.m. At that time, several special drones would crash into Maria's mansion. This would be followed by several other drones carrying explosives to destroy the mansion. The drones would be backed up by three attack helos from the Navy Base in Key West. In addition to backing up the helicopters, there were several Coast Guard ships located in the Gulf and the Atlantic sides of the island. DPS and several other military helicopters would be in the area to deploy additional manpower and equipment if necessary.

The sheriff interrupted O'Neill. He told his officers to raise our right hands and had a federal judge deputize all of us as federal police officers. This meant that we were now acting under federal jurisdiction. After everyone in the conference room had done this, O'Neill moved into the next phase.

Several squads of police and O'Neill's elite personnel would converge on the mansion. O'Neill's personnel would go in first, the rest of the response teams would wait until the mansion was secured, and we would move in to execute search warrants and arrest those left. The drones would attack at 2:00 a.m. followed by O'Neill's men; then the other responses teams would move into the clean-up phase. The operation should be over by 3:30 a.m.

Once Doaks heard this, he could not contain himself. He stood up and interrupted the briefing. "Listen, Commander, with all due respect, you are wrong on your time assessment. You have not seen or participated in what this woman can do. First she probably knows about this plan. Remember she took on thirty of our SWAT team members from our department and DPS. Then she escaped without being noticed. Her planning on counterattacking our men was incredible. I believe that, given your plan, she will know exactly the time of the attack and what to expect. She also will have any weapon defense possible to stop the attack. Your use of drones and all of this technology needs to be researched more—she knows what we have, and she knows when we are coming."

He was about to continue when O'Neill stopped him. "Are you saying that this battle plan that was just drawn up—Maria knows about this already?"

"Yes, she does. She has people everywhere, including here. I can guarantee that she knows what you are planning and has a counterattack planned. Listen, all I am saying is that I have experienced her battlefield tactics twice. She always knows what is coming and how to counteract any attack. I have lost many good cops, and I am telling you to do more research on your plan and change everything!" With that, Doaks sat down.

Bourne was just about to jump up and tear Doaks' head off when O'Neill told him, "Please sit down, and let's talk." For the next few minutes, the room was deathly silent. No one spoke. All eyes were on O'Neill. Then he spoke.

"First, thank you, Sergeant Doaks, for your opinion. I appreciate your insight and your experience in responding to our plans. But this operation will go on as scheduled, and I believe Maria has never had the full force of our technology thrown at her. I respect your opinion, but I am going through with this operation as planned. Now, you can either decide to support us, or you can leave the room—so what is it?"

Doaks turned red. I thought he was going to stroke out, but, to his credit, he shook his head and said, "Thank you! I am staying!" Then the briefing continued.

After the briefing, I was heading back to my office when Doaks grabbed my arm and told us we were going out. He then ordered me to jump into his vehicle. There he told me in a hushed voice, "I have made contact with a mole at Maria's hideout. His name is Pedro. He has leaked information to me in the past when Maria or one of her bosses was going to take out a cop or other government official. He contacted me last night and wants to meet. He told me he has critical information he just learned from Maria about our attack plans. He wants to share this with me and you for a price. We are going to meet him now. FYI—I shared this information with O'Neill and Clutch prior to our briefing. Both wanted to go ahead with the briefing as scheduled. Once we are done with Pedro, we are going to meet with the sheriff, O'Neill, and Clutch and alter our attack plans."

After leaving HQ, we turned onto a deserted road on the Gulf side of Marathon. There we got out of the car, and Doaks motioned me to follow him. We entered an abandoned-looking garage where a person was waiting. The person was standing in the shadows as Doaks came through the doorway.

"Pedro, Pedro, it's Doaks! Don't shoot!" Doaks moved into the light from the window. I was right behind him, gun drawn. Pedro came out of the shadows holding an MP-5. Doaks told him, "Put it down. The girl is my partner. Put it down." Pedro lowered his weapon and looked about twelve years old. Doaks told me to holster my weapon and let Pedro talk.

Pedro confessed that he had hated being part of Maria's gang since he was ten. Maria had promised to promote him into a territory boss's position, and she had promised him a lot of money. She had done nothing on these promises, but she had killed his girlfriend. Several months ago, Maria had given Pedro some new experimental drugs—drugs she told Pedro he should try out with his friends, then report back to her on the results. Pedro took them back to his girlfriend. They partied with the drugs that night; then, while lying in his arms, she told him she was pregnant with his baby then the drugs killed her. Pedro looked into her eyes and promised her he would kill Maria.

I was still wrapping my head around this conversation when Doaks asked, "What is Maria planning?"

Pedro then laid out an incredible defense for all of the things O'Neill had been planning. Pedro spoke of some type of netting that would be placed outside the perimeter of the mansion, then over the roof of the mansion. He continued explaining how Maria had some type of electronic device that could jam any radio signals on any type of drones the government would be using in their attacks. He also explained that she had acquired a number of shoulder-fired rockets to bring down either boats or aircraft in the area. He talked about some type of experimental gun that she had purchased that could fire at any target. Doaks asked if this gun had a name. Pedro thought for a second, then stated that she called it a *rail gun* or something like that. Doaks let him finish. Pedro also said she had discussed strategy with his cousin, El Jefe. El Jefe told him that if they were not winning the battle, they would escape via a small submarine she had docked under the mansion. Maria stated this submarine was unique—and fast.

She said they could be in Cuba in three hours.

Doaks was now twitching. He looked at Pedro and asked, "Why should I believe any of this?"

"Because I have already disabled the netting devices. I expect she may figure that out, but by the time your guys start the attack, it will be too late. And besides, I want to see the *bruja* dead. She killed my future wife and my child. She needs to die, and I want to personally kill her!"

"Pedro, does she have information on the time of the attack or the use of drones in the attack or anything else?"

Pedro shook his head and told Doaks and me the exact time of the attack discussed in our earlier briefing. He also told us that Maria knew the attack plan using the drones. I immediately thought, *How does Maria continue to have spies in our department?* Then he asked Doaks, "Where is the money?" *Well, that was expected*, I thought. Doaks handed him a brown envelope. Pedro put down his weapon and looked inside. "Is it all there?"

"Yes, $50,000 cash. And remember to have your cell phone on when we attack so you can send me the locations of Maria, Patron, and Jefe once the attack begins. One other thing, put this on your head prior to the attack. This headband will save your life. I will make sure that everyone in this raid knows who you are and what headband you are wearing." Doaks shook his head, looked at me, and said, "I knew it! That d - -m Maria still has spies in our department!" Doaks thanked Pedro, and we all left.

Doaks and I headed back to Rosa's for lunch. I was stunned at Doaks' actions over the past forty minutes or so. "How in the heck did you find this guy, Pedro, and where in the world did you come up with that kind of money?" I asked.

"Well, never underestimate me, Rookie," he said, tapping his temple. "All up here!"

"What are you going to do next?" I asked.

"You'll see," he said as he pulled into Rosa's for lunch. We entered Rosa's but did not go to the main dining area. Instead Doaks went to a side room near the restrooms. There he opened a door and, at a small table, were the sheriff, O'Neill, Bourne, and Clutch.

All of them stood when we came into the room. "Success?" the sheriff asked.

Doaks nodded. "Yes. Let's eat, and I will debrief you." After coffee and tacos, Doaks went over everything Pedro had told him. To my surprise, everyone in the room nodded their heads and thanked Doaks for his actions.

"You have probably saved dozens of cops' lives and my elite teams' lives today," O'Neill said. "Thank you!" He offered Doaks his hand.

Bourne then took over the lunch, stating, "OK, we are a go for tonight. We hit this place at 12:30 a.m. Any questions?" *Wow*, I thought, *I'm glad we are moving up the operation.* O'Neill and the rest of the men got up and left via the outside entrance. Doaks and I remained.

I took a long drink of water, then turned to him. "How

long have you been planning this?" I asked.

"About a few days ago, I ran through some old case files looking for someone I could turn on Maria. I remembered the homicide case involving Pedro and his girlfriend. I did some research on where he was living, contacted him a few days ago, and made him an offer. As you saw, he accepted my offer, and now we can finally get that woman!"

October 27—The attack

At 12:30 a.m. a small robot-type device rolled down the roadway to the mansion. Then, in a loud voice, it told anyone in the area, "This is the police! Open the door, come out with your hands up, and you will not be hurt." That was met with a few rounds from an automatic weapon; then all h - -l broke loose. The drones hit the house on all sides, other drones attacked the three or four machine gun nests, and one drone hit the basement dock where the submarine was anchored. The battle looked like it was over when, like a phoenix rising out of the ashes, Maria counterattacked.

Her drones hit our vehicles like she knew exactly where we had parked our cars. Her people used shoulder-fired missiles to take out two of our helos; however, two Cobra attack copters eliminated any possibility of any more helos going down. Finally, after twenty more minutes of gunfire, drone attacks on both sides, and the explosion of some type of bomb in an area where this suspected rail gun was located, a white flag appeared out of the wrecked front door. I was with Doaks. We were hidden behind a stone wall when we saw the flag. *Is it over*, I thought.

Doaks and I were just about to stand up when we saw O'Neill's men approaching the front doorway. Just as several people were coming out, a claymore mine exploded—then several more. Seconds later, all of O'Neill's men were down, and all of the suspects appeared to have been killed. Then one more individual came out blazing away at anyone moving south of the driveway. In one shot, that person was down. Then I heard O'Neill telling his commander on the radio to commence a cleanup operation. I wasn't sure what that meant, but within seconds several of O'Neill's units converged on the mansion. Shots and explosions continued for the next thirty minutes.

Finally, one of the men in his unit brought Pedro back to our command post. Pedro was slightly wounded, but he recognized Doaks and immediately began to talk. He told Doaks that Maria, Patron, and Jefe had left via a secret doorway and disappeared. Doaks, having known about the submarine, alerted O'Neill. Bourne jumped in and told O'Neill to tell the Navy officers to release the "package." I stood back and wondered, *What the heck is the package?* I found out later that the package was a new submarine hunter drone, designed to locate and sink any type of submarine. The package was a prototype, and this was its first trial. The package was released, and five minutes later, we all heard a muffled "crump" sound.

"That's it! We sunk the sub!" Bourne yelled.

"Not so fast," Doaks and I said together. He went on, "We assume that Maria is still alive and well until we confirm she is dead, and we see her body." Just after he said these words, two things happened. First, the command vehicle I was standing in front of blew up. Then I blacked out. When I came to, I saw Doaks on the ground in front of me, with Bourne and O'Neill to my left. Then behind me another vehicle blew up. I tried to crawl toward Doaks, but my body wouldn't move. I grabbed my radio and put out an Officer Down call—then I passed out again.

Five minutes later, I was being lifted up. I wrestled with whomever was lifting me. I opened my eyes to see O'Neill. He dragged me to another safe area, where I started to come around. I looked at him, then kissed him. "Are you OK?" I asked.

"I got a little scratch on my right leg," he told me, then he sank to his knees and passed out.

"Crap!" I said and yelled for medics to get to my location. I looked at O'Neill's right leg, then applied a tourniquet to it. He had a deep wound bleeding out. I had to stop the bleeding, or he would lose his leg. I got my belt around his leg, stopped the bleeding, and yelled into my radio again, "Where the h - -l is the medic?" I was about to get up when the first of three medics showed up. Two of them got O'Neill, loaded him onto a stretcher, and left. One looked at me and asked, "Are you hurt anywhere?"

"No, I'm shaken up, but all my parts are working. Please come with me. My partner is over there, and he needs your help." We started moving when a burst of automatic weapons erupted west of our location. "Who the heck is firing at us?" I yelled to the medic.

"I don't know, but stay on the ground and crawl over to my partner." In the next few minutes, two drones hit the location where the weapons fire occurred. Then there was silence.

When we reached Doaks, he wasn't breathing. I rolled him over and began CPR. The medic took over, and I again yelled into my radio, "I needed more medics at my location!" The medic was still performing CPR on Doaks when I prayed to God, "Please save him!" Two minutes later, Doaks was still not responding. Two other paramedics arrived and loaded Doaks on a stretcher. I was going to go with him when the paramedics stopped me.

Then I heard Doaks yelling, "Rookie, get that b - - h!"

"Yes, sir!" I yelled back at him and took off toward the mansion. I entered the basement and was stopped by one of O'Neill's men.

"What are you doing here?" he asked.

"I am looking for the woman responsible for all of this." I pulled out a picture of Maria Hernandez. "Have you found her, or her body, anywhere in this place yet?" The man shook his head. That was all I needed. I told him to get his squad and come with me. I was going to find this woman if it was the last thing I ever did.

For the next fifteen minutes—which seemed like years—we searched the entire basement area. I told all of the men to look for a fake doorway or passage or something unusual. I told them how Maria had escaped through a hidden hallway in another battle, and I believed she had an opportunity here. We were still hunting in the basement when I heard a noise in the room adjacent to me. I motioned to several of the squad members to follow me and put my finger to my lips. "Let's be very quiet," I whispered. I went through the closed door first, then the rest of the team followed. I was twenty feet into the room when the claymore on a delayed switch exploded. I was thrown to the ground, while all of O'Neill's men were motionless behind me. "Damn!" I yelled.

Then I looked up and saw her—Maria—trying to jump into a strange-looking boat. I jumped to my feet and ran at her. She saw me and turned to fire a weapon, but I was immediately firing every round in my Glock at her. I reloaded on the run and continued to fire. One more time, I reloaded and continued firing. I saw her go down into the boat. Then I saw the boat slowly moving into the Gulf and hit a buoy. The boat exploded and, once more, I hit the ground. I got up, radioed my position, and requested a Coast Guard boat at my location ASAP.

Miraculously one of the Coast Guard response boats was at my location in seconds. I jumped on board and told the sailor to go to the location where the boat was smoking and submerged in the water. As we got closer to the boat, I saw

Maria. We arrived on scene, and I had my gun ready to shoot her again. I looked into the remains of the boat—and there was Maria, lying at the bottom. She had a number of bullet holes in her. The boat was partially submerged in the Gulf. She was bleeding out; blood was all over the boat and in the water. She looked at me and smiled. Then, as she was reaching for her weapon, a large shark grabbed her by the head and pulled her into the Gulf.

"*Adios, bruja!*" I yelled at her. I radioed our location to some other officers; they could do the crime scene processing. I left the scene to check on O'Neill and Doaks.

Epilogue

October 30, 2021

A few days later, I was dispatched to the west shore of Vaca Cut. There a fisherman had reported seeing a human arm and leg washed up on shore under the bridge. I responded and found a human arm and leg. I processed the crime scene and submitted the parts to Dr. Spock. He called me a few hours later to confirm that these human parts belonged to the *late* Maria Hernandez. He confirmed that it was Maria by running her fingerprints through our state's AFIS. The results came within four hours and verified that the prints were hers. "Finally," I whispered to myself—"she is dead!"

After getting the verification on Maria's death, I returned to the hospital to see how Doaks, O'Neill, and Bourne were recovering. Doaks was still in ICU. He was not doing well. O'Neill was up but under the influence of pain meds because of the extensive surgery on his right leg. Bourne had been released earlier that day. He probably was already helping the Navy or Marines on some other project.

I found O'Neill's doctor and asked him, "What's the prognosis on O'Neill?"

"I doubt he will ever be able to walk again, he lost most of his leg during that battle, we did the best we good putting it back into one piece. " Hearing this, I left the ICU waiting area and went down to the hospital chapel to pray again. I asked God for hope. Hope that Doaks would live. Hope that O'Neill would walk again. And hope for us. I had prayed that the good Lord would provide me with the right man to marry. And now I knew that the right man was O'Neill.

I was just about to leave when the sheriff entered the chapel. "Hood, Doaks is crashing, and the doctor just found a moving blood clot in O'Neill's femoral artery. Please come…"

Coming in 2024... *The Hope*

Does Doaks die? Does O'Neill live, and will he ever walk? Will Katie and O'Neill get married? Are the objects and coins found by Todd and Shane from the *Isabella*? What will the DNA results from the two babies show? More bodies of women are being found in isolated areas in Key Marathon—who is killing them? Has a serial killer returned to the area? Has another criminal element returned to Key Marathon to replace Maria Hernandez's crime organization?

These questions and others will be solved in the next book, completing the trilogy: *The Hope*.

You can follow Dr. H as *The Hope* is written by going to his website: harryhueston.com.

Made in United States
Troutdale, OR
03/18/2025